D1011822

Dear Reader,

A PIECE OF TEXAS is a ne̶̶̶̶̶̶̶̶̶̶̶̶
close to my heart. Each book is linked by a group of fictional
soldiers, who served together during the Vietnam War, and a
piece of a deed to a ranch each was given before going off to
war. Although the focus of each story is on the next generation
of one of the soldiers' family members, I did quite a bit of
research on the Vietnam War. Most of the research wasn't
necessary, as each story takes place in the present time, but I
was determined to learn as much about the experiences and the
lives of the soldiers who served there.

Although I grew up on the fringes of the Vietnam War—it
was being fought during my high school and college years—
I knew very little about the war and was, for the most part,
untouched by it…until I married a Vietnam vet. My husband
was a Green Beret in the United States Army and was a part of
the MACV-SOG (Military Assistance Command, Vietnam—
Studies and Observation Group), an unconventional warfare
task force engaged in highly classified operations throughout
Southeast Asia. Throughout our marriage, he talked very little
about the time he spent in Vietnam, and only recently began
sharing more and more of his experiences there. I never
understood his reluctance to discuss his experiences and I'm
not sure that he could, either, if he were asked, but I have a
feeling it was a means of self-preservation.

It's been thirty-five years since my husband returned from
Vietnam and it was only this past year that he was willing
to visit the Vietnam Memorial in Washington, D.C. It
was a very emotional experience for him, as names of
many of the men he served with are carved on the wall.
David "Babysan" Davidson, the soldier whom this book
is dedicated to, is one of those names.

I hope you enjoy reading this series, and I hope, too,
that through the small peeks I've offered of the soldiers'
experiences, you might gain a better appreciation for the men
in the armed forces who put their lives on the line for our
country each and every day.

Peggy Moreland

Dear Reader,

This April, leave the showers behind and embrace the warmth found only in a Silhouette Desire novel. First off is Susan Crosby's *The Forbidden Twin*, the latest installment in the scintillating continuity THE ELLIOTTS. This time, bad girl twin Scarlet sets her heart on seducing the one man she can't have. And speaking of wanting what you can't have, Peggy Moreland's *The Texan's Forbidden Affair* begins a brand-new series for this *USA TODAY* bestselling author. A PIECE OF TEXAS introduces a fabulous Lone Star legacy and stories that will stay with you long after the book is done.

Also launching this month is Maureen Child's SUMMER OF SECRETS, a trilogy about three handsome-as-sin cousins who are in for a season of scandalous revelations...and it all starts with *Expecting Lonergan's Baby*. Katherine Garbera wraps up her WHAT HAPPENS IN VEGAS...series with *Their Million-Dollar Night*. What woman could resist a millionaire who doesn't care about her past as long as she's willing to share his bed?

Making her Silhouette Desire debut this month is Silhouette Intimate Moments and HQN Books author Catherine Mann, with *Baby, I'm Yours*. Her delectable hero is certainly one guy this heroine should think about saying "I do" to once that pregnancy test comes back positive. And rounding out the month with a story of long-denied passion and shocking secrets is Anne Marie Winston's *The Soldier's Seduction*.

Enjoy all we have to offer this month!

Melissa Jeglinski

Melissa Jeglinski
Senior Editor
Silhouette Desire

Please address questions and book requests to:
Silhouette Reader Service
U.S.: 3010 Walden Ave., P.O. Box 1325, Buffalo, NY 14269
Canadian: P.O. Box 609, Fort Erie, Ont. L2A 5X3

PEGGY MORELAND

The Texan's Forbidden Affair

Silhouette®

Desire

Published by Silhouette Books
America's Publisher of Contemporary Romance

If you purchased this book without a cover you should be aware that this book is stolen property. It was reported as "unsold and destroyed" to the publisher, and neither the author nor the publisher has received any payment for this "stripped book."

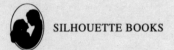

SILHOUETTE BOOKS

ISBN 0-373-76718-8

THE TEXAN'S FORBIDDEN AFFAIR

Copyright © 2006 by Peggy Bozeman Morse

All rights reserved. Except for use in any review, the reproduction or utilization of this work in whole or in part in any form by any electronic, mechanical or other means, now known or hereafter invented, including xerography, photocopying and recording, or in any information storage or retrieval system, is forbidden without the written permission of the editorial office, Silhouette Books, 233 Broadway, New York, NY 10279 U.S.A.

All characters in this book have no existence outside the imagination of the author and have no relation whatsoever to anyone bearing the same name or names. They are not even distantly inspired by any individual known or unknown to the author, and all incidents are pure invention.

This edition published by arrangement with Harlequin Books S.A.

® and TM are trademarks of Harlequin Books S.A., used under license. Trademarks indicated with ® are registered in the United States Patent and Trademark Office, the Canadian Trade Marks Office and in other countries.

Visit Silhouette Books at www.eHarlequin.com

Printed in U.S.A.

PEGGY MORELAND

published her first romance with Silhouette Books in 1989 and continues to delight readers with stories set in her home state of Texas. Winner of the National Readers' Choice Award, a nominee for the *Romantic Times BOOKclub* Reviewer's Choice Award and a two-time finalist for the prestigious RITA® Award, Peggy's books frequently appear on the *USA TODAY* and Waldenbooks bestseller lists. When not writing, Peggy can usually be found outside, tending the cattle, goats and other critters on the ranch she shares with her husband. You may write to Peggy at P.O. Box 1099, Florence, TX 76527-1099, or e-mail her at peggy@peggymoreland.com.

Dedicated to the memory of
David Arthur Davidson
"Babysan"
Staff Sergeant
Special Forces
United States Army
March 8, 1947–October 6, 1971

Prologue

Older men declare war. But it is the youth that must fight and die.

—Herbert Hoover

June 14, 1971

It was a hell of a way for a man to spend his last night in the States. Given a choice, Larry Blair would have preferred to be curled up in bed with his wife rather than sitting in a smoke-filled bar watching his buddies get drunk.

But the Army wasn't into choices. Larry's orders were to report to San Francisco International Airport, 15 June at 0500. Five new soldiers assigned to his platoon—all Texas boys—had agreed to meet on Monday in Austin, Texas, to catch a late flight to San Francisco. There they would board yet another plane for the last leg of their journey.

Destination: Vietnam.

Larry looked around at the guys seated at the table. Fast Eddie. T.J. Preacher. Poncho. Romeo. Those weren't their real names, of course. Real names were all but forgotten two days after hitting boot camp and replaced with one better suited to the guy's personality. Since meeting up with the soldiers, Larry had lost one handle—Tex—and received another—Pops. He supposed the new one was a better fit, since he was the oldest member of the group.

He shook his head sadly. Twenty-one and the oldest. Proof enough of the youth and inexperience of the soldiers fighting this damn war.

He narrowed his eyes thoughtfully as he studied the soldiers sitting at the table, wondering if a one of them had a clue what he would be in for once he reached 'Nam.

He sure as hell did. Unlike the others, this was his second tour of duty in 'Nam. When he'd completed his first assignment, he'd re-upped for another six months. At the time it had seemed like the thing to do. In many ways Vietnam was a young man's wet dream. Whores, booze and drugs for the taking, plus the adrenaline high that came with engaging in combat and the thrill of cheating death one more day. With no family waiting for him back home, no job to return to, he'd thought, *Why not roll the dice and stay another six months?*

But during the thirty-day leave he'd received as a bonus for re-upping, he'd met and fallen in love with

Janine Porter and married her two weeks later. Now he'd give his right arm to be able to erase his name from that dotted line. He had a wife, and that was a damn good reason to stay alive.

But like they say, he thought, lifting his beer in acknowledgment of the old adage, *hindsight is twenty-twenty.*

Before he could take a sip, Romeo scraped back his chair and headed for the bar and a woman seated there. The soldiers remaining at the table immediately began laying bets as to whether or not he would score. Larry didn't bother to reach for his wallet. If what he'd heard about Romeo's reputation was true, the lady didn't stand a chance. According to the guys who'd gone through basic training with him, Romeo could charm the panties off a nun and receive them as a souvenir afterward.

A shadow fell across the table, and Larry glanced over his shoulder to find a man standing behind him.

"You soldiers headed for Vietnam?" the stranger asked.

Larry hesitated a moment, unsure of the man's purpose in approaching him. Americans' view of the Vietnam war varied, and he'd been called everything from a hero to a murderer. But he wasn't ashamed of the uniform he wore or the job he was doing for his country. And he sure as hell wasn't one to back down from a fight, if pushed.

Scraping back his chair, he stood, his head high, his shoulders square. "Yes, sir. We're catching a plane for San Francisco tonight, then shipping out for 'Nam tomorrow."

The man nodded, his expression turning grave. "Thought so. My son served in 'Nam."

Relieved that the man didn't appear to be looking for trouble, Larry asked, "What branch of the service was he in?"

"Army. Didn't wait for the draft to get him. Volunteered fresh out of high school."

"What's his name? Maybe I know him. This'll be my second tour."

"Walt Webber," the man replied, then shook his head sadly. "But I doubt you'd know him. He was killed in '68. Stepped on a mine four days before he was supposed to leave for home."

Larry nodded soberly, having heard similar stories. "I'm sorry for your loss, sir. A lot of good men didn't make it home."

The man nodded, then forced a smile and offered his hand. "I'm Walt Sr., though I reckon the *senior*'s no longer necessary."

Larry gripped the man's hand firmly in his own. "I'm pleased to meet you, sir. Larry Blair."

Walt shifted his gaze and nodded toward the others gathered around the table. "I'd consider it an honor if you'd let me buy you and your friends a drink."

Larry dragged up another chair. "Only if you'll join us."

The man's face lit with pleasure at the invitation. "Why, thank you, son. It's been a while since I've had the opportunity to spend time with any young folks."

After they were seated, Larry introduced Walt to the others, then gestured to the bar where Romeo was still sweet-talking the lady. "And that's Romeo," he explained. "He's with us, too."

"Romeo," Walt repeated, then chuckled. "Looks like the name fits."

Smiling, Larry nodded his agreement. "Yes, sir, it does."

Walt bought a round of drinks for everyone, then bought another round when Romeo returned, after losing his chance of scoring with his lady friend when her husband showed up. He received a good razzing from those who had lost money on the bet, then conversation at the table dwindled.

Walt studied the soldiers as they nursed their drinks. "You boys scared?" he asked bluntly.

Preacher, the meekest of the bunch and probably the most honest, was the first to respond. "Yes, sir," he admitted. "I've never shot a man before. Not sure I can."

"I 'magine you'll find it easy enough once those Vietcong start shooting at you," Walt assured him.

"Maybe," Preacher replied, though his expression remained doubtful.

Walt took a sip of his drink, then set it down and sighed. "Hell of a war. From what my son told me, it's like fighting ghosts. The Vietcong hit hard, then slip back over the border into the safe zone where the Americans can't touch them."

"True enough," Larry agreed. "To make matters worse, it's hard to tell who's the enemy. Old men. Women. Children. They all pose a threat, as they're just as likely to be carrying a gun or grenade as the Vietcong soldiers."

Walt nodded. "My son said the same thing. Claimed the number of casualties reported is nothing compared to the number of soldiers who've been maimed by booby traps or mines." He set his mouth in a grim line. "That's what got Walt Jr. After he stepped on that mine, there was nothing left of him but pieces to ship home."

Larry saw the shadow of sadness in the man's eyes and knew Walt was still grieving for his son. But there was nothing he could say to ease the man's sorrow. All he could do was listen.

"He was my only son," Walt went on. "Only child, for that matter. We lost his mother to cancer when he was in grade school, and with her all hope of having any more children. Walt Jr. was planning to work the ranch with me when he got out of the service. We were going to be partners." He dragged a sleeve across the moisture that filled his eyes. "Won't be doing that now."

Every soldier at the table ducked his head, obviously uncomfortable with witnessing a grown man's tears. But Larry couldn't look away. He understood Walt's grief. He may not have lost a son to the war, but he'd lost friends. Good friends. Friends whose memories he'd carry with him until the day he died.

He clasped a hand on the man's shoulder. "Your son was fortunate to have a father who cared so much for him."

Walt glanced at Larry and their eyes met, held a long moment. "Thank you, son," he said quietly, then swallowed hard. "My only hope is he knew how much I loved him. I never was one for expressing my feelings much."

Larry gave Walt's shoulder a reassuring squeeze before releasing it. "He knew," he assured him. "Words aren't always necessary."

Firming his mouth, Walt nodded as if comforted by the assurance, then forced a smile and looked around the table. "So. What do you boys plan to do when you get back home?"

Romeo shrugged. "Beats me. Haven't thought that far ahead."

"Same here," T.J. said, and the others nodded their agreement.

Walt glanced at Larry. "What about you?"

Larry frowned thoughtfully. "I'm not sure. I've never done anything but soldiering. Signed up right out of high school, intending to make a career of it." He smiled sheepishly. "But I got married a couple of weeks ago and that's changed things considerably. Army life is hard on a family. Once I finish up this tour, I'm hoping to find myself a new career, one that'll allow me to stay closer to home."

"Ever done any ranching?" Walt asked.

Larry choked a laugh. "Uh, no, sir, can't say that I have."

Walt glanced at the others. "How about y'all?"

Romeo smoothed a hand down his chest and preened. "I have. One summer, my old man cut a deal with a buddy of his for me to work on a ranch. Figured it would keep me out of trouble."

"Did it?" Walt asked.

Romeo shot him a sly look. "Depends on what you call trouble."

His reply drew a laugh from the soldiers at the table, as well as from Walt.

"Tell you what," Walt said. "Since my son can't be my partner on the ranch, why don't the six of you take his place? Everybody gets an equal share, and when I pass on, the ranch will be yours."

For a moment Larry could only stare. Was the man drunk? Crazy? Nobody just up and gave a ranch to total strangers. "Uh, that's awfully nice of you," he said hesitantly, "but we couldn't accept a gift like that."

"Why not?" Walt asked indignantly. "It's mine to give to whoever I want, and it just so happens I want you boys to have it."

Larry glanced at the others at the table, reluctant to voice his concerns out loud. "With all due respect, sir, there's no guarantee we'll make it home either."

Walt shot him a confident wink. "I'm bettin' you will." He slipped a hand into his shirt pocket and pulled out a folded sheet of paper and a pen. After spreading the paper open on the table, he began to write.

"This here is a bill of sale," he explained as he wrote. "I'm naming each one of you as part owner in the Cedar Ridge Ranch."

"But we don't know anything about ranching," Larry reminded him.

Walt waved away his concern. "Doesn't matter. I can teach you boys everything you need to know."

When he'd completed the document, he stood and shouted to the occupants of the bar, "Anybody here a notary public?"

A woman seated at a table on the far side of the room lifted her hand. "I am."

"Have you got your seal on you?" he asked.

She picked up her purse and gave it a pat. "Just like American Express. Never leave home without it."

He waved her over. "Come on, then. I need you to notarize something for me."

When she reached the table, Walt explained that he wanted her to witness the soldiers signing the document, then make it official by applying her seal. After

she nodded her assent, he passed the piece of paper to
T.J., who sat at his left. "Sign your name right here," he
instructed, pointing.

T.J. hesitated a moment, then shrugged and scrawled
his name. The piece of paper passed from man to man
until it reached Larry.

Larry looked at Walt doubtfully. "Are you sure
about this?"

"Never more sure of anything in my life," Walt
replied. He shot Larry another wink. "I'll share a little
secret with you. On the last tax appraisal the Cedar
Ridge Ranch was valued at three million. Y'all knowing
that you're part owners in a place like that is going to
give you boys a reason to stay alive."

Three million dollars? Larry thought in amazement.
He'd never seen that kind of money in his life! He
puffed his cheeks and blew out a long breath, then
thought, *What the hell,* and added his name to the
bottom of the page.

After verifying that all appeared legal, Walt took the
document and tore it into six pieces. He lined them up
on the table. "Now it's your turn," he informed the
notary public. "Sign your name on each and stamp 'em
with your seal."

Though Larry could tell the woman was as stunned
by Walt's generosity as he was, she dutifully signed her
name on each slip of paper, then pulled her embosser
from her purse and applied the official seal.

When she was done, Walt gathered up the pieces.
"Keep this someplace safe," he instructed the soldiers
as he handed each a section of the torn document.
"When your tour of duty is up, you boys put the bill of

sale back together and come to the Cedar Ridge and claim your ranch."

Larry stared at the scrap of paper a moment, unable to believe this was really happening. Giving his head a shake, he slipped the paper into his shirt pocket, then extended his hand to Walt. "Thank you, sir."

Smiling, Walt grasped his hand. "The pleasure's all mine." He stood and tucked the pen into his shirt pocket. "I reckon I better head for home. It's too late for an old man like me to be out." He leveled a finger that encompassed all the soldiers. "Now you boys be careful, you hear?" he warned, then grinned. "Y'all've got yourselves a ranch to run when you get home."

One

Stephanie Calloway had always prided herself on her ability to handle even the most complex situations with both efficiency and calm. As one of the most sought-after photo stylists in Dallas, Texas, those two traits were crucial to her success. On any given day she juggled six-figure budgets, kept track of prop inventories valued sometimes in the millions, and coordinated the schedules of the photographers, models and assistant stylists assigned to a particular shoot. If requested, she could transform an empty corner of a photographer's studio into a beach on the Caribbean, outfit a dozen models in swimwear to populate the space, then tear it all down and create an entirely different setting on the whim of a hard-to-please client.

So why, when faced with the task of disassembling and disposing of the houseful of items her parents had accumulated during their thirty years of marriage, did she feel so overwhelmed, so inadequate, so utterly *helpless?*

Because this is personal, she reminded herself as she looked around the den of her childhood home. Each item in the room represented a massive mountain of emotion she feared she'd never find the strength to climb.

"And standing here dreading it isn't accomplishing a thing," she told Runt, the dog at her side.

Taking a deep breath, she crossed to her father's recliner and laid a hand on its headrest. Oh, how he'd loved his recliner, she thought as she smoothed a hand over the impression his body had worn into the leather. When he wasn't out working on the ranch, he could usually be found reared back in the chair, with one of his dogs curled on his lap. He'd always had a dog tagging along with him, Runt being his most recent… and his last.

As if aware of her thoughts, Runt nudged his nose at her knee and whined low in his throat. Blinking back tears, she looked down at him and gave him a pat, knowing by his soulful expression that he was missing her father as much as she was. Runt—the name her father had given him because he was the runt of the litter—wasn't a runt any longer, she noted. The top of his head struck her leg at midthigh. Part Australian sheepdog and part Labrador retriever, he had inherited traits from both breeds, resulting in an intelligent long-haired dog with a sweet temper. But a long line of other canines had preceded him, and not all had been as endearing as Runt. Biting back a smile, she dipped her head in search of the section of frayed upholstery at the recliner's base, compliments of Mugsy—a Jack Russell terrier—and made during a chewing stage her mother had feared would never end.

The tears rose again at the thought of her mother, and she glanced over at the overstuffed chair positioned close to the recliner. Though her mother had preceded her father in death by two years, the floor lamp at its right remained angled to shed light on her hands and the endless knitting projects she worked on at night. An afghan for the church auction. A warm shawl for one of the ladies at the nursing home. A sweater for Stephanie.

Her chin trembled as she envisioned her mother and father sitting side by side, as was their habit each night, her mother's knitting needles clicking an accompaniment to the sound of whatever television program her father had tuned in at the moment.

How will I ever get through this alone? she asked herself, then sagged her shoulders, knowing she had no other choice. With no siblings to share the responsibility, the job was hers to do.

Releasing a shuddery breath, she said, "Come on, Runt," and forced herself to walk on.

They made it as far as the hallway before she was stopped again, this time by a gallery of pictures depicting her family's life. Her gaze settled on a photo of her and her father taken at a Girl Scout banquet when she was eleven. Few would guess by the proud swell of his chest that Bud Calloway was her stepfather and not her natural father. From the moment Bud had married her mother, he'd accepted Stephanie as his own and had assumed the full duties of a father. Never once in all the years that followed had he ever complained or made her feel as if she were a burden. She touched a finger to the glass, his image blurred by her tears. She was going to miss him. Oh, God, she was going to miss him so much.

Gulping back the grief, she tore her gaze away. She had taken no more than two steps when Runt stopped and growled. Linking her fingers through his collar to hold him in place, she glanced back over her shoulder. She strained, listening, and tensed when she heard the familiar squeak of hinges that signified the opening of the front door. Since she hadn't told anyone of her plans, she wasn't expecting any visitors—especially one who could get past a locked door. Mindful that burglars sometimes read the obituaries in search of vacant homes to rob, she whispered to Runt, "I hope your bite is as ferocious as your growl," and cautiously retraced her steps, keeping a firm hold on his collar.

As she approached the doorway that opened to the entry, she caught a glimpse of a man standing just inside the door. She might've screamed if she hadn't immediately recognized him. The thick sandy-brown hair that flipped up slightly at his ears, just brushing the brim of his cowboy hat. The tall, lanky frame and wide shoulders. The faded chambray shirt, jeans and scuffed cowboy boots.

No, she had no problem recognizing him. As she'd learned the hard way, Wade Parker was a hard man to forget.

Runt whined, struggling to break free. At the sound, Wade whipped his head around and his gaze slammed into Stephanie's. As she stared into the blue depths, she felt the old familiar tug of yearning and forced steel into her spine, pushing it back.

Runt wriggled free and leaped, bracing his front paws on Wade's chest.

Smiling, Wade scrubbed his ears. "Hey, Runt. How you doin', boy?"

She advanced a step, her body rigid with anger. "What are you doing here?"

The smile Wade had offered Runt slid into a frown. Urging the dog down to all fours, he gestured at the front window. "Drapes were open. Since they're usually closed—or have been since Bud's funeral—I figured I'd better check things out. Didn't see a car. If I had, I would've knocked."

"I parked in the garage," she informed him, then narrowed her eyes to slits. "How did you get in? The door was locked."

"I didn't break in, if that's what you're suggesting. Bud gave me a key after your mother passed away. Figured someone close by should have one in case anything happened to him and needed to get inside the house."

She thrust out her hand. "There's no need for you to have a key any longer. Bud's gone."

He whipped off his hat. "Dang it, Steph!" he said, slapping the hat against his thigh in frustration. "Do you intend to spend the rest of your life hating me?"

She jutted her chin. "If emotion ends with death, yes, at least that long."

Scowling, he tucked his hat beneath his arm and dug a ring of keys from his pocket. "I thought you went back to Dallas after the funeral," he grumbled.

"Only long enough to tie up a few loose ends."

He worked a key from the loop. "So how long are you planning on staying?"

"That's none of your business."

He slapped the key on her palm and burned her with a look. "Maybe not, but Bud's cattle *are*."

She drew back to peer at him in confusion. "But I assumed Mr. Vickers was taking care of the cattle. He always helped Dad out in the past."

He snorted and stuffed the key ring back into his pocket. "Shows how much you know. Vickers moved to Houston over a year ago. When Bud got to where he couldn't do his chores himself, I offered to do them for him."

Her eyes shot wide. "*You* worked for my father?"

"No," he replied, then added, "Not for pay, at any rate. I offered, he accepted. That's what neighbors do."

She stared, stunned that her father would accept anything, even a favor, from Wade Parker. "I…I had no idea."

"You might've if you'd ever bothered to come home."

She jerked up her chin, refusing to allow him to make her feel guilty for not visiting her father more often. "Dad and I talked on the phone three or four times a week."

He snorted. "That was mighty nice of you to squeeze him into your busy schedule."

His sarcasm rankled, but before she could form a scathing comeback, he held up a hand.

"Look," he said, suddenly looking tired. "I didn't come here to fight with you. I only came to check on the cattle."

She wanted to tell him that she didn't need his help, that she would take care of the livestock herself. But it had been years since she'd done any ranch work, and she wasn't at all sure she could handle the job alone.

She tipped up her chin. "Hopefully I'll be able to free you of that obligation soon. When I finish clearing out the house, I'm putting the ranch on the market."

He dropped his gaze and nodded. "Bud said he didn't think you'd keep the place."

She choked a laugh. "And why would I? I have no use for a ranch."

He glanced up and met her gaze for a long moment. "No, I doubt you would." He reached for the door-knob, preparing to leave. "Have you talked to Bud's attorney?"

She trailed him to the door. "Briefly. We're supposed to meet after I finish clearing out the house." She frowned. "Why do you ask?"

He lifted a shoulder as he stepped out onto the porch. "No reason. If you need anything—"

"I won't."

Her curt refusal dragged him to a stop at the edge of the porch. Dropping his chin, he plucked at the brim of his hat as if he had something to say but was having a hard time finding the words. Seconds ticked by, made longer by the silence, before he finally spoke.

"Steph…I'm sorry."

Scowling, she gave Runt's collar a firm tug to haul him back inside and closed the door without replying.

As far as she was concerned, the apology came years too late.

Wade exited the barn and headed for the house, exhausted after the long hours he'd put in that day. No, he mentally corrected. His exhaustion wasn't due to the amount of time he'd worked or the effort expended. His weariness was a result of his run-in with Steph. The woman frustrated the hell out of him and had for years.

He knew it was his fault she felt the way she did about him, but what the hell had she expected him to do? He'd made a mistake—a big one—and had tried his best to rectify it by doing what was *right*. In doing so, he'd hurt Steph. But dammit, he'd suffered, too. He wondered sometimes if she realized how much.

As he neared the house, music blasted from the open windows, the bass so loud it reverberated through the soles of his boots and made his teeth ache. Stifling a groan, he made a quick detour to his toolshed. He wasn't in the mood for another argument and he knew if he went inside now he was bound to wind up in one. Meghan called that junk she listened to hip-hop. He considered it trash and had forbidden her to play it. Unfortunately she hadn't docilely bowed to his wishes. Instead she'd screamed and cried, accusing him of ruining her life—which was nothing new, since she accused him of that at least once a day.

He slammed the door of the toolhouse behind him and succeeded in muffling the sound of the irritating music only marginally. Sinking down on an old nail keg, he buried his face in his hands. How the hell was a father supposed to deal with a rebellious daughter? he asked himself miserably. If Meghan were a boy, he'd take her out behind the woodshed and give her a good spanking, the same as his father had when Wade had disobeyed the rules. A few swats on the behind had made a believer out of Wade, and he figured it would Meghan, too…if he could bring himself to spank her.

Groaning, he dropped his head back against the wall.

When had his life gotten so screwed up? he asked himself. There was a time when his daughter had idolized him, thought he all but walked on water. Not so any longer. In fact, she'd told him on more than one occasion that she hated his guts and wished she could go and live with her mother. There were days when he was tempted to pack her bags.

He shook his head, knowing full well he'd never allow Meghan to live with Angela. Hell, that was why he'd fought so hard for custody of his daughter in the first place! Angela wasn't fit to be a mother. Even the judge, who historically ruled in favor of mothers, had recognized Angela's deficiencies and awarded Wade custody of Meghan.

No, Wade wasn't going to allow Meghan to browbeat him into letting her go and live with her mother. He'd deal with her rebellion, the same as he'd dealt with every other stage of her development. But damn, he wished there was someone to share the responsibility with, someone he could at least talk to about his problems with his daughter! He'd give his right arm to be able to sit across the table from his mom and dad right now and seek the wisdom of their years and experience as parents.

But his parents were gone, he reminded himself, victims of a random murder, according to the police. Random or not, his parents were dead, and the car-jacker who had killed them was currently sitting on death row.

He'd taken the loss of his parents hard—and inheriting the millions they'd left him had in no way softened the blow. If anything, it had only made things worse. He had been twenty-two at the time of their deaths and living on his own. After he'd buried his parents, he'd gone kind of crazy and done some things he wasn't too true proud of. He'd quickly discovered that when a man has money to burn, there's always somebody around offering to light the match. *Bottom-feeders,* his dad would've called them. Folks who thrived on another person's misery.

He still wasn't sure what it was that had made him realize he was traveling on a fast train to nowhere. But one morning he'd looked at himself in the mirror and was ashamed of what he'd seen. In a desperate attempt to put his life back together, he'd pulled up roots and bought the ranch in Georgetown, hoping to make a fresh start.

Less than two months after the move, he'd met Steph. He hadn't been looking for romance the day he'd delivered the bull to the Calloway ranch. In fact, romance had been the furthest thing from his mind. But it was on that fateful day that he'd met his neighbors' daughter, home for summer break between semesters. He remembered when Bud had introduced her to him how her smile had seemed to light up her entire face, how her green eyes had sparkled with a sense of humor and innocence that he'd envied. And he remembered, when he'd shaken her hand, how delicate yet confident her fingers had felt in his. By the time he'd left several hours later, he had been head over boot heels in infatuation and already thinking of ways to see her again.

From their first date on, they'd spent almost every waking minute together. With a ranch to run, Wade hadn't had a lot of time to spare for formal dates. But Steph hadn't seemed to mind. She'd ridden along with him when he'd needed to check his fences, sat with him in the barn through the night when his mare had foaled. She'd brought him lunch to the field when he was cutting hay and sat with him beneath the shade of an old oak tree, laughing and talking with him while he ate.

When summer had come to an end and it was time for her to go back to college, he had stood with her parents and watched her drive away, feeling as though a boulder were wedged in his throat. Before the first week was out he knew he couldn't live without her. That very weekend he'd taken his mother's wedding ring out of the safe where he'd kept it and headed for Dallas to propose.

In his mind's eye he could see Steph as she'd looked that day. He hadn't told her he was coming, and when she'd spotted him standing in the parking lot of her apartment complex, her eyes had widened in surprise, then she had broken into a run, her arms thrown wide. With a trust and openness that warmed his heart, she'd flung herself into his arms and he'd spun her around and around. He remembered the way she'd tasted when he'd kissed her, the weight of her in his arms. And he could still see the awe in her expression when he'd given her the ring, the love and tears that had gleamed in her eyes when she'd looked up at him and given him her answer. It was a memory he'd carry with him to his grave.

But dwelling on the past wasn't going to help him deal with his daughter, he told himself. Knowing that, he braced his hands against his thighs and pushed himself to his feet and headed for the house, already dreading the ugly scene that awaited him.

* * *

Stephanie didn't give another thought to her encounter with Wade Parker. As she'd learned to do with any unpleasantness, she blocked it from her mind and focused instead on something more productive—in this case, cleaning out her parents' home. It helped to know that the sooner she finished the job, the sooner she could leave Georgetown and close this chapter of her life once and for all.

She had started with the dining room, thinking that, as the only formal room in the house, it would hold fewer personal possessions, fewer memories. Wrong! After two days spent purging and packing, she'd already filled all the storage boxes she'd brought with her from Dallas...and emptied two boxes of tissues mopping her tears. It seemed everything held a memory, from her mother's silver tea service to the chipped ceramic Cookies for Santa plate that had graced their hearth every Christmas for as far back as Stephanie could remember.

Fully aware that this job was going to be tough, she had attempted to disassociate herself from the personal aspects attached to it by applying an organizational tool she'd picked up while watching HGTV. She had created three areas—Keeper, Trash and Donate—and set to work.

Sadly, after two days of what she'd considered cold-blooded sorting, the Keeper stack of boxes towered over the other two.

Promising herself that she would be more ruthless in her decision making, she tried to think where she could find more boxes. She was sure there were probably some in the attic, but the attic had always given her the willies.

Unfortunately the only other option was driving into town, and that prospect held even less appeal. Thirteen years later, and she still felt the sting of the pitying glances from people she'd once counted as friends.

With a sigh of resignation she turned for the hallway and the narrow staircase at its end, with Runt tagging along at her heels. It took some muscle to open the door at the top of the stairs, and once inside, her knees turned to rubber when she was confronted with the sheet-draped objects and cobwebs that filled the space.

She remembered well the last time she'd entered this room. She'd been ten years old and sent there by her mother to retrieve a box of canning jars. While searching for the requested box, one of the sheets had billowed as if someone was trying to fight free from beneath it. Convinced that she was about to be attacked by a band of killer ghosts, she'd run back down the stairs screaming bloody murder. Though her mother had assured her there were no such things as ghosts, from that day forward Stephanie had refused to step foot in the attic again.

Narrowing her eyes, she studied the sheet-draped objects, trying to remember which one had frightened her that day. *That one,* she decided, settling her gaze on a hump-shaped object in the corner. Determined to confront her fear and dispel it, she murmured a firm, "Stay" to Runt, then marched across the room and lifted the sheet.

Half expecting a ghost to come flying out, when nothing but dust motes rose in the air, she gave a sigh of relief and flung back the sheet to expose an old steamer trunk. Never having seen the trunk before, intrigued, she lifted the lid. Another sheet, this one free of dust, protected the truck's contents. Beneath it she found a variety of boxes, each tied with string. Her curiosity piqued, she selected the largest box and sat down on the floor, anxious to see what was inside. After removing the lid, she folded back the tissue paper.

She clapped a hand over her heart. "Oh, my God," she murmured as she stared at the Army uniform folded neatly inside. Sure that it was her father's, she gently lifted the jacket and held it up to examine it more closely. A name tag attached above the breast pocket read Sgt. Lawrence E. Blair.

"Oh, my God," she whispered, awed by the sight.

Unaware that her mother had saved anything that belonged to her biological father, she shoved the box aside and pulled out another. After quickly untying the string, she lifted the lid. Bundles of letters, each bound with pink ribbon faded to a dusty rose, filled the space. She thumbed through the envelopes, noting that each was addressed to Janine Blair. Though the months of the postmarks varied, all were mailed in the same year, 1971. Stunned by her discovery, she pulled out another box, then another, and found more letters in each.

She stared at the stacks of letters scattered around her, unable to believe that her mother had never told her of their existence. Was it because the memories were too painful? she asked herself. Or was it because her mother had chosen to bury the memories of her first husband along with his body?

She knew her parents' marriage had been impulsive, spawned by him leaving for the war. She remembered her mother telling her that he'd shipped out for Vietnam just two weeks after they were married. But Stephanie

really didn't know much else about her natural father—
other than his name, of course, and that he had been
killed in the war. She remembered asking her mother
once if she had any pictures of him, and she'd claimed
she hadn't.

Wondering if her mother had secreted away pictures
along with the letters, she pushed to her knees and dug
through the box until she found what looked to be a
photo album. Hopeful that she would find pictures of
her father inside, she sank back down and opened the
book over her lap.

The first photo all but stole her breath. The picture
was a professional shot of a soldier and probably taken
after he'd completed his basic training, judging by his
buzzed haircut. He was wearing a dress uniform and
had his hat angled low on his forehead. The name tag
above the breast pocket identified him as Lawrence E.
Blair.

He looks so young, was all she could think. And so
handsome. She smoothed her fingers over his image.
This is my father, she told herself and waited for the
swell of emotion.

But she felt nothing. The man was a stranger to her.
Her *father,* yet a complete stranger.

Emotion came then, an unexpected guilt that stabbed
deeply. She should feel something. If she didn't, who
would? His parents had preceded him in death. Her
mother—his wife—was gone now, too. There was no
one left to remember him, to mourn for a life lost so
young.

Along with the guilt came another emotion—resentment toward her mother. *Mom should have shown me this*

trunk, she thought angrily. She should have made sure that I knew my father, that his memory lived on in my heart. He had courageously served his country and fathered a child he'd never seen. Surely he deserved more than a trunk full of memories tucked away in an attic.

Firming her jaw, she pushed to her feet and began gathering up the boxes. She would read the letters he left behind, she told herself. She'd get to know him through his correspondence and the album of pictures. She wouldn't let his memory die. He was her father, for God's sake, the man who had given her life!

Two

Later that night, as Stephanie passed through the kitchen dragging the last bag of trash she'd filled that day, the house phone rang. She didn't even slow down. It was her parents' phone, after all; anyone who wanted to speak to her would call her on her cell.

Ignoring the incessant ringing, she strong-armed the bag through the opening of the back door, then heaved it onto the growing pile at the foot of the steps. Winded, she dropped down on the top step to catch her breath.

Although the sun had set more than an hour before, a full moon lit the night sky and illuminated the landscape. From her vantage point on the porch she could see the roof of the barn and a portion of the corral that surrounded it. Beyond the barn stretched the pastures where the cattle grazed. Though she couldn't see the cattle, she heard their low bawling and knew they were near. Runt let out a sharp bark, and she winced, feeling guilty for having banished him to the barn. But it was for his own good, she told herself. She'd seen a mouse earlier that day and had set out traps. Runt, God love him, had already activated two—due to his curiosity or greed, she wasn't sure which—and had a bloody nose to prove it.

Knowing that spending one night in the barn wouldn't hurt him, in spite of the pitiful look he'd given her when she'd penned him there, she let the peacefulness of her surroundings slip over her again.

Though raised on the ranch, she'd spent her adult years surrounded by the big-city noises of Dallas and had forgotten the depth of the quiet in the country. Closing her eyes, she listened closely, separating the sounds of the night: the raspy song of katydids perched high in the trees, the closer and more melodious chirping of crickets. A quail added its plaintive call of "bob-white" to the chorus of music, and she smiled, remembering the first time she'd heard the call and asking Bud who Bob White was and was that his mommy calling him home.

Enjoying the quiet and the pleasant memories it drew, she lay back on the wooden planks of the porch and stared up at the sky, letting her mind drift as she watched the clouds float across the face of the moon.

Her earliest memories were rooted here on this ranch, she thought wistfully. Prior to her mother marrying Bud, she and her mother had lived with her mother's parents in town. Stephanie had vague recollections of that time, but she wasn't sure if they were truly hers or a result of images she'd drawn from stories her mother had shared with her of those early years. A natural storyteller, her mother had often entertained Stephanie with tales of when Stephanie was a little girl.

But she'd never told her any that had included Stephanie's father.

The resentment she'd discovered earlier returned to burn through her again. Why, Mom? she cried silently. Why didn't you tell me anything about him? Why did you refuse to talk about him when I asked questions? Was he funny? Serious? What kind of things did he enjoy? What were his fears?

Her cell phone vibrated, making her jump, and she quickly sat up, pulling it from the clip at the waist of her shorts. She flipped up the cover to check the number displayed on the screen and recognized it as Kiki's, her assistant.

Swiping at the tears, she placed the phone to her ear. "Kiki, what are you doing calling me?" she scolded good-naturedly. "You're supposed to be on vacation."

"Vacation?" Kiki repeated. "Ha! Being stuck at home with three-year-old twins isn't a vacation, it's a prison sentence!"

Laughing, Stephanie propped her elbow on her knee, grateful for the distraction Kiki offered from her whirling emotions. Five foot nothing, Kiki had flaming red hair that corkscrewed in every direction and the personality to match it. Talking to her was always a treat. "Don't you dare talk about my godchildren that way. Morgan and Mariah are angels."

"Humph. Easy for you to say. You haven't been locked up in a house with them all day."

"Wanna trade places?" Stephanie challenged. "I'd much rather be with the twins than doing what I'm doing."

Kiki made a sympathetic noise. "How's it going? Are you making any progress?"

Stephanie sighed wearily. "None that you'd notice. I had no idea my parents had so much stuff. I've spent three days in the dining room alone and I'm still not done."

"Found any hidden treasure?"

Stephanie thought of the trunk in the attic and the letters and photos she'd found hidden inside. "Maybe," she replied vaguely, unsure if she was ready to talk about that yet.

"Maybe?" Kiki repeated, her voice sharpening with interest. "Spill your guts, girl, I'm desperate for excitement."

Chuckling, Stephanie pushed the hair back from her face and held it against her head. "I doubt you'd find a bunch of old letters and a photo album that belonged to my father all that exciting."

"You never know," Kiki replied mysteriously. "Bud could've had a wild side we weren't aware of."

"They weren't Bud's. They belonged to my real father."

There was a moment of stunned silence. "Oh, wow," Kiki murmured. "I forget that Bud had adopted you."

"I do, too, most of the time, which is what I'm sure Mom intended."

Although Stephanie wasn't aware of the bitterness in her tone, Kiki—who never missed anything—picked up on it immediately.

"What gives? You sound majorly ticked."

"I'm not," Stephanie said defensively, then admitted grudgingly, "Well, maybe a little." She balled her hand into a fist against her thigh, struck again by her mother's deception. "I can't believe she never told me she saved any of his things. She kept it all hidden away in a trunk in the attic."

"Why?"

"How would I know? She just *did*."

"Bummer," Kiki said sympathetically, then forced a positive note to her voice. "But, hey, the good news is you found it! Have you read any of the letters yet?"

Stephanie had to set her jaw to fight back the tears that threatened. "No, but I'm going to read every darn one of them. Somebody's got to keep his memory alive."

"Are you okay?" Kiki asked in concern. "You sound all weepy—and you *never* cry."

Stephanie bit her lip, resisting the urge to tell Kiki everything, from the resentment she felt over her mother's deception to seeing Wade again. "I'm fine," she assured her friend. "I'm just tired."

"Cleaning out your parents' home is hard enough, and now you gotta deal with all this heavy stuff about your dad. Do you want me to come and help?"

Stephanie smiled at the offer, knowing Kiki would drop everything and drive to Georgetown if asked. She was that kind of friend. "No, I can handle it. But thanks."

"Well, I mean it," Kiki assured her. "You say the word and I'm there."

Stephanie chuckled, imagining how much work they'd get done with the twins underfoot. "Thanks, but I've got everything under control. You just caught me at a weak moment. Listen," she said, anxious to end the call before she caved and begged Kiki to come. "It's getting late. I'd better go. Give the kids a kiss for me, okay?"

"I will. And take things slow," Kiki urged. "If it takes

you longer than two weeks to finalize things there, so what? The advertising industry won't collapse without us. Once you get back home, we can work doubly hard to make up for any time lost."

Stephanie pressed her fingertips to her lips, fighting back the tears, realizing how lucky she was to have a friend like Kiki.

"Thanks, Kiki," she said, then added a hasty goodnight and disconnected the call before Kiki could say anything more.

Within fifteen minutes of ending the call with Kiki, Stephanie was in bed, propped up on pillows, the bundles of her father's letters piled around her. She'd already sobbed her way through two and was reaching for a third when the house phone rang. She angled her head to frown at the extension on the beside table. It was the second time the phone had rung since she'd talked to Kiki, and the sound was beginning to grate on her nerves.

Since her parents were a decade or more behind technology and didn't have caller ID installed on their phone line, she couldn't check to see who was calling. And she wasn't about to answer the phone just to satisfy her curiosity. At this hour, she doubted the caller would be a telemarketer, which meant that one of her parents' friends had probably heard that she was at the house and was calling to offer his or her condolences over the loss of Bud.

Considering her current emotional state, Stephanie was afraid that one kind word would send her into a crying jag she wouldn't be able to stop.

After the fifth ring, the ringing stopped. With a sigh

of relief Stephanie sank back against pillows and opened the letter over her propped-up knees.

Dear Janine,
It's been a crummy day. Rain, rain and more rain. Sometimes it seems like it's never going to stop. This is the third day we've been guarding this LZ (that's Landing Zone to you civilians), and everything I own is sopping wet—including my underwear. Ha-ha.

I got your letter before I left camp. The one where you asked about getting a dog? Honey, that's fine with me. In fact, I'd feel better knowing you have something (not someone!) to keep you company while I'm gone. What kind do you want to get? Make sure it's something that'll make a good guard dog. Not one of those sissy poodles. They are about as useless as tits on a nun.

"Tits on a nun?" she repeated, then choked a laugh. Obviously her father *had* possessed a sense of humor. Pleased to discover that small detail about his personality, she settled in to read more.

Have I told you that I love you? Probably about a million times, but it's worth repeating. I miss you so much it hurts.

Stephanie placed a hand over her heart, knowing exactly how he must have felt. She'd experienced that depth of feeling only once in her life, and though it was more than a decade ago, she remembered it as if it were yesterday. A love so powerful it was a physical pain in her chest. Even now, after years with no contact, thoughts of Wade would occasionally slip unbidden into her mind and she would experience that same deep ache. Thankfully all she had to do was remind herself of what a jerk he'd turned out to be and the feeling would disappear as rapidly as it had come.

She gave her head a shake to clear the distracting thoughts and focused again on the letter, picking up where she'd left off.

I know I probably shouldn't tell you that because it'll only make you sad, but it's the truth. I'd give anything to be holding you right now. Sometimes at night I close my eyes real tight and concentrate real hard on imagining you. A couple of times I swear I thought I even smelled you. Crazy, huh? But it's true. That perfume you wear really turns me on. Remind me to buy you a gallon of it when I get home!

I better sign off for now. It's getting so dark I can't see, and we can't turn on so much as a flashlight when we're out in the field because it might give our position away. Man, I'll be glad when this damn war is over!
Yours forever,
Larry

Stephanie stared at the letter a long time, trying to absorb the words he'd written and what he'd revealed about himself through them. It was obvious that he'd loved her mother very much and was concerned for her welfare. Had her mother's feelings for him equaled his for her? Unsure of the answer, pensive, she refolded the letter and selected another from the pile.

Dear Janine,
I'm going to be a daddy?

Stephanie sat bolt upright, her eyes riveted on the words, realizing that she was holding the letter her father had sent after learning that her mother was pregnant. She squeezed her eyes shut, afraid to read any more. What if he was disappointed that her mother had gotten pregnant so soon after their marriage? Even mad? He may not have wanted any children.

"Please, God, let him have wanted me," she prayed fervently, then opened her eyes and read on.

Whoa. That's some pretty serious sh** to throw on a guy when he's halfway around the world. Don't think I'm not happy about it, because I am! I'm just disappointed that I'm stuck over here and not there with you. The good news is, if my calculations are right, I should be home by the time our baby is born.

"Oh, God," Stephanie murmured and had to stop reading to wipe her eyes. He not only had wanted her, he'd been looking forward to being home in time for her birth. The irony of that was simply too cruel for words. Blinking hard to clear her eyes, she scanned to find her place and began to read again.

*Are you feeling okay? I know women sometimes
throw up a lot in the beginning. I sure hope you're
not one of those who stays sick for nine months.
Are you showing yet? That's probably a crazy
question, since you can't be that far along. I'll bet
you look really sexy pregnant!*

*Man, I can't believe this! Me, a daddy! It's
going to take a while for this to really sink in. As
soon as I get home, we're going to have to find a
place of our own. I'm really glad that you're there
with your parents so they can take care of you
while I'm gone, but when I get home I want you
all to myself! Does that sound selfish? Hell, I
don't care if it does! I miss you like crazy and
don't want to share you with anybody, not even
your mom and dad!*

*We'll need a place with lots of room, because
I want a whole houseful of kids. We never talked
about that, but I hope you do, too. I don't want our
baby growing up without any brothers or sisters
the way I did. Believe me, it can get pretty lone-
some at times.*

*You mentioned in your letter that, for my sake,
you hope it's a boy. Honey, I don't care what we
have. I'll love our baby no matter what.*

*Preacher just walked by and I told him our
good news—I hope you don't mind. He said to
tell you congratulations. Remember me telling
you about Preacher? He's the one who didn't
think he could shoot a man. So far he's squeaked
by without having to. I'm worried that if it ever
comes down to shoot or die, he won't be able to*

*pull the trigger. I try my best to keep an eye on
him, but it's hard to do that when things get
really hot, with enemy fire coming at us from
every direction.*

*I better sign off for now. I've got to find
somebody who's got a pass to town and see if
he'll bring me back a box of Cuban cigars. I've
got some celebrating to do!*
Love forever,
Larry

Unable to keep the tears in check any longer, Stephanie dropped her forehead to her knees and wept. She
cried for a life lost so young, for the brave young man
who'd worried about his friend and was willing to put
his friend's safety above his own.

And she cried selfish tears at the injustice of never
having gotten to know her father, tears of anger at her
mother for not sharing her memories of him with her.

And she cried for the love her father had felt for her
mother, a love that he had carried to his grave with him,
a love snuffed out before it had had time to fully bloom.

And when she would've thought there were no tears
left, she cried for her own lost love and the dreams
she'd once built around Wade Parker and the life they
might have shared together. A love, like her father's, that
was snuffed out before it could fully bloom.

Muttering curses under his breath, Wade slammed
the door of his truck behind him and cranked the engine.
He wasn't in the mood to go chasing across the coun-
tryside playing the Good Samaritan. Not when his head

was still aching from going three rounds with his daughter over the proper attire for a girl her age.

Swearing again at the reminder of the argument, he stomped the accelerator and aimed the nose of his truck for the highway. Like he had a clue about women's fashion, he thought irritably. But he knew one thing for certain: no daughter of his was going out in public wearing a shirt cut six inches above her belly button and jeans that rode so low on her hips they barely covered her privates!

Where did kids come up with these crazy ideas anyway? he asked himself, then snorted, already knowing the answer. Television, that's where. And the worst were those asinine reality shows. Hell, there was nothing real about a one of 'em! And even if there was, what was the fun in *watching* reality when all a person had to do to experience it firsthand was get off his or her duff and take a stroll outside?

Feeling his blood beginning to boil again, he forced his fingers to relax from the death grip he had on the steering wheel and refocused his mind to the problem at hand. And Steph *was* a problem, whether she was aware of it or not. And thanks to a telephone call from a complete stranger, she was now *his* problem. He supposed he could've refused the lady's request that he check on Steph, but then he would've had to live with the guilt—and he was already carrying a full load. He didn't know how long he was going to be required to make atonement before he was able to clear his conscience of what he'd done to Steph. Judging by the fact that he was driving down the road in the middle of the night, when he should've been sacked out in bed, it appeared it wasn't going to be anytime soon.

He'd thought a phone call would be the easiest and least aggravating method of accomplishing the duty dumped on him. Forget that he'd already tried to call her once that evening, on his own volition, and hadn't received a response. Still, he'd tried again—twice, to be exact. Receiving no answer either time, there was nothing to do but make the drive to the Calloways' ranch and make sure she was all right. For all he knew, she could've fallen off a ladder and broken a leg and was unable to get to the phone.

As he pulled to a stop behind her SUV, he noticed that the windows on the house were dark. Good, he thought smugly and strode to the door. He hoped she was in bed and he awakened her, so that he could ruin her sleep, the same as she was ruining his. He knocked, then waited a full two minutes before knocking again. When he still didn't receive a response, he frowned, wondering if she really had injured herself. Though he figured she was going to be madder than a hornet with him for using it, he lifted a hand above the door and felt along the ledge for the key Bud kept hidden there. Finding it, he dealt with the lock and pushed open the door.

"Steph?" he called as he stepped into the entry. "Are you here?" He waited a moment, listening, and frowned when he didn't hear a reply.

"Steph," he called again and flipped on the overhead light.

God almighty, he thought in dismay as he looked around. The place looked as if a tornado had passed through it! Boxes were stacked on the floor and against the wall. In the dining room, the doors of the china cabinet stood open, its shelves stripped bare. Sheets of newspaper draped the back of the chairs and littered the floor, and more boxes lined the walls. The table itself was covered with stacks of dishes and whatnots a foot deep.

Shaking his head, he turned for the den. Not seeing any sign of Steph amongst the debris in that room, he continued down the hall. A muffled sound came from the rear of the house, and he followed it to the door of what he knew was her old childhood bedroom. Opening the door a crack, he peeked inside and found her sitting on the bed, her face buried in a pillow she held on her lap.

He hesitated, not wanting to disturb what he assumed was a private moment of grief. But the heart-wrenching sound of her sobs pulled him into the room.

"Steph?" he said quietly. "Are you okay?"

She snapped up her head, exposing a face streaked with tears. She stared, her face pale and her eyes wide, as if she were looking at a ghost.

Realizing too late that he'd probably scared her half to death, he held up his hands. "I didn't mean to scare you. I called a couple of times, and when you didn't answer, I was worried you might've hurt yourself and couldn't get to the phone."

She turned her face away, swiping at the tears. "I'm fine. I wasn't in the mood to talk to anyone."

She wasn't physically hurt, that much was obvious, but as to being fine, he had his doubts. If her swollen eyes were any indication, it appeared she'd been crying for hours and wasn't through yet.

He shifted from one foot to the other, anxious to get out of there but reluctant to leave her in her current emotional state. "I can hang around for a while, if you want," he offered hesitantly.

"That's not necessary."

Though she kept her face turned away, he heard the tears in her voice and knew she was still crying. Silently cursing her stubbornness, he crossed the room and sat down on the edge of the bed.

"I know you're missing Bud," he said gently. "I miss him, too."

She kept her face turned away but shook her head. "It—it's not Bud." She hitched a breath and lifted a hand in which she held what appeared to be a letter. "It's from my f-father."

He stared at the back of her head in confusion. Had she lost her mind? Bud *was* her father. "Bud left you a letter?" he asked, hoping to snap her back to her senses.

She shook her head in frustration. "N-not Bud. M-my *real* father."

He hesitated a moment, then reached for the phone. "Maybe I should call a doctor."

Before he could lift the receiver, she clamped her hand over his wrist.

"I don't need a doctor," she said through bared teeth. "Bud was my *step*father!" Releasing her grip on him, she fell back against the pillows and covered her face with her hands.

Wade stared, trying to make sense of what she'd said. "Bud adopted you?"

Though she kept her face covered, she bobbed her head, letting him know he'd assumed correctly.

He slowly unwound his fingers from the receiver. "But…who's your real father?"

"Larry Blair." Drawing in a deep breath, she dragged her hands from her face. "He—he was killed in Vietnam."

Wade rubbed a hand across the back of his neck. "I always assumed Bud was your father."

"Which is obviously what my mother wanted."

He drew back to peer at her, surprised by the venom in her voice. "And what's that supposed to mean?"

She pushed a foot against one of the bundles scattered over the bed. "These are all letters from my father. I found them, along with a photo album, in the attic."

"So? What does that have to do with your mother?"

"I never knew they existed! She never told me."

Stunned by her level of anger, he tried to think of a logical explanation to offer. "Maybe she did and you forgot."

"Oh, no," she said, shaking her head in denial. "I didn't forget. I distinctly remember asking her if she had a picture of him and her claiming she hadn't saved any of his things. She never wanted to talk about him. Ever." She banged a fist against her thigh, her eyes filling with tears again. "She lied to me. My own mother *lied* to me!"

He held up a hand. "Now, don't go assuming the worst. Could be she was only trying to protect you."

"From *what?*" she cried, her voice rising in hysteria. "My heritage? From the opportunity to know the man who fathered me?"

"No, from being hurt." He tipped his head toward the letter she clutched. "Obviously reading his letters has upset you. Your mother probably knew they would and wanted to save you the pain."

"She had no right. He was my father, for God's

sake! Can you imagine what it's like not knowing anything about your father? To know that he died without
ever seeing you? He was excited when Mom told him
she was pregnant with me." She thrust the letter in
front of his face and shook it. "It says so right here. He
wanted me!"

Reluctant to comment one way or the other for fear of
setting her off again, he said vaguely, "I'm sure he did."

She dropped her hands to her lap, her shoulders
sagging dejectedly. "Never mind. You wouldn't understand. I'm not even sure that I do."

She dragged in a long breath, then released it and forced
a polite smile. "I appreciate you coming to check on me,
but there's no need for you to stay any longer. I'm fine."

As badly as Wade would've liked to hightail it out
of there and leave her to wallow in her misery alone,
there was no way in hell he could do that. Not and be
able to live with his conscience later.

"No rush. I can stick around for a while."

She flattened her lips, all sign of politeness gone. "Then
let me make myself a little clearer. I don't want you here."

He lifted a shoulder. "I guess that makes us even,
'cause I don't particularly want to be here either."

She tossed up her hands. "Then make us both happy
and *leave!*"

He shook his head. "Can't. Leavin' might make me
happy, but I suspect it's not gonna help you any."

Her eyes narrowed to slits. "Wanna bet?"

He hid a smile, having forgotten how feisty Steph
could get when riled. Seeing her exhibit that particular
trait made him realize that he'd succeeded in getting her
mind off her sadness for a while. Pleased with himself,

he bumped his shoulder against hers, making room for himself to sit beside her on the bed.

"What do you think you're doing?" she asked incredulously as he stretched his legs out alongside hers.

He folded his hands behind his head. "Gettin' comfortable. Looks like you're needin' to unload some emotional baggage." He lifted a shoulder. "Since I'm willin' to listen, I figure I might as well make myself comfortable."

She rolled to her knees, her eyes dark with fury as she faced him. "If and when I think I need a shrink, I'll hire one."

Ignoring her, he picked up an envelope and pulled out the letter it held. "What branch of the service was your father in? Navy?"

"Army," she snapped. "And you're not staying."

He scanned a few lines and glanced over at her. "Have you read this one yet?"

She folded her arms across her chest and pressed her lips together.

He bit back a smile. "I'll take that as a no. Probably best if you didn't," he advised and slipped the pages back into the envelope. "There are some things about her parents' life that a daughter is better off not knowing."

She snatched the envelope from his hand and pulled out the letter. He watched her eyes widen as she skimmed the first page.

"I tried to warn you," he said, trying not to laugh.

Her cheeks flaming, she stuffed the pages back into the envelope. "You did that on purpose," she accused.

He opened his hands. "How was I supposed to know

that letter was gonna have graphic descriptions of your parents' sex life?"

She burned him with a look before burying the letter at the bottom of the stack. "You could've just set it aside and said nothing. Saying what you did was the same as daring me to read it."

"You'd have gotten around to reading it eventually," he reminded her. "I was just trying to save you the embarrassment." He cocked his head and frowned thoughtfully. "Do you think it's really possible to do it in a—"

She held up a hand. "Please. I don't need that particular visual in my head."

"Why were you crying?"

She blinked at the sudden change of subject, then let her hand drop. "I don't know," she said miserably. "It's just all so sad. There's no one left but me to remember him, yet I know nothing about him."

He picked up a bundle of letters and bounced them thoughtfully on his palm. "And this is how you plan to get to know him?"

"It's all I have."

He studied the bundle a moment. "I guess you know you're setting yourself up for a lot of pain." He shifted his gaze to hers and added, "And probably an equal share of embarrassment. What he wrote in these letters was meant for your mother's eye, and hers alone."

She nodded tearfully. "I realize that, but this is all I have that was his. Reading his letters is my only way of learning about him."

His expression grave, he set the bundle aside. "I want you to promise me something."

"What?"

"Promise that you'll call me whenever you feel the need to talk."

"No, I—"

He pressed a finger against her lips, silencing her. "You helped me through a hard time after I lost my parents. I think I deserve the chance to even the score."

He could tell that she wanted to refuse his request, but she finally dropped her chin to her chest and nodded. He figured she was only agreeing so she could get rid of him, but that was okay. He knew how to make sure she kept her end of the deal.

With that in mind, he swung his legs over the side of the bed and picked up an empty box from the floor. Using the length of his arm, he raked the bundles of letters inside.

Her mouth gaped open. "What are you doing?"

He hitched the box on his hip—and out of her reach. "Helping you keep your promise. Every afternoon, when I come over to feed the cattle, I'll drop off a bundle of letters for you to read. After I'm done feeding, I'll stop back by and check on you. That way I'll know if you're honoring your promise."

"What will seeing me prove?"

"One look at your face and I'll know whether or not you need to talk."

She opened her mouth, then clamped it shut, obviously realizing it was useless to argue with him.

His job done for the moment, he turned for the door.

"Wait!"

He stopped and glanced over his shoulder to find her eyeing him suspiciously.

"How did you get inside the house? I made you return the key Bud gave you."

"I used the one he kept hidden above the front door."

Her eyes shot wide. "You knew about that?"

He lifted a brow. "Oh, I think you'd be amazed at all I know."

Three

The next morning Stephanie stormed around the house, stripping pictures off the walls and stacking them against the wall in the dining room. It was the only packing she trusted herself to do while in a blind rage.

She couldn't believe she'd agreed to Wade's ridiculous arrangement. Having him dole out her father's letters to her was demeaning enough, but then to be subjected to his perusal so that he could judge her mental and emotional state was masochistic! She didn't want to share her thoughts and feelings with him. She'd die a happy woman if she never had to *see* him again!

Hearing his truck stop out front, she groaned, then set her jaw and marched to the door. Before he could even knock, she yanked open the door, snatched the bundle of letters from his hand and slammed the door in his face, turned the lock. Pleased with herself for outsmarting him, she hurried to the den and settled into her mother's chair.

She had just pulled the ribbon, releasing the bow that held the stack of letters together, when the hair on the back of her neck prickled. Sensing she was being watched, she glanced toward the doorway and nearly jumped out of her skin when she found Wade standing in the opening.

He dangled the house key between two fingers. "Nice try," he congratulated her. "Too bad it didn't work."

His smile smug, he slipped the key into his pocket, letting her know in his not-so-subtle way that attempting to lock him out in the future would be a waste of her time, then touched a finger to the brim of his hat in farewell.

"I'll be back as soon as I finish feeding the cattle," he called over his shoulder before closing the door behind him.

Mentally kicking herself for not thinking to remove the hidden key, Stephanie scooped up the scattered letters and rapped them into a neat stack on her lap. She should have known that a locked door wouldn't stop Wade Parker. The man could all but drip sugar when it suited him and rivaled Attila the Hun when he wanted his way.

Her smile turning as smug as the one he'd gifted her with while dangling the key in her face, she plucked a letter from the top of the stack. Well, two can play this game as well as one, she told herself as she smoothed open the creased pages. She knew how to compartmentalize her emotions, if and when the situation required it. When Wade returned to check on her, he'd find her dry-eyed and busy packing. She wouldn't give him any reason to think she needed to "unload," as he'd referred to her emotional state the previous night.

Confident that she could outsmart him, she began to read.

Janine,
Have you ever had the feeling that everybody in the world is going crazy and you're the only sane person left? That's how I feel right now. I swear, a couple of guys in my unit have gone nuts. If they're not drunk, they're smoking grass—or worse.

Out in the field, we work as a unit and depend on each other to stay alive. But these guys are so out of it most of the time, I can't trust them to cover my back. I tried talking to them, told them the booze and drugs were messing with their heads and that they were going to get us all killed if they didn't cut that crap out. They just laughed and called me an old man and worse. Hell, I don't care what they call me. I just don't want their stupidity getting them—or any of the rest of us—killed.

Sorry. I didn't mean to go off like that and I sure as heck don't want to make you worry. Sometimes I just need to unload—

Stephanie pursed her lips at the word *unload*, wishing her father had chosen a term other than the one Wade had used to describe her need to talk. Giving the pages a firm snap, she began to read again.

but there's nobody that I can talk to about this stuff. If I go to the lieutenant, I'll feel like a rat for squealing and probably get my buddies in trouble.
Enough of this. Telling you about it isn't going

*to change things any. How are you feeling? Has
the morning sickness passed yet? How much
weight have you gained? And don't worry about
those extra pounds. It just gives me more to love!
Have you thought of any names yet? If it's a boy,
we could name him William, after my father, and
call him Will for short. And if it's a girl, I've
always liked the name Stephanie. I knew a girl
once—not a girlfriend, just a friend—named
Stephanie, and she was really cool. Stephanie
Blair. How does that sound?*

*Better go. The chopper is due soon to pick up
the mail, and I want this letter to be on it when
it takes off.*
Love forever,
Larry

Stephanie carefully refolded the letter and slipped it
back into the envelope. He had named her. Her father,
not her mother, had chosen her name. She quickly
sniffed back the emotion that realization drew.

See, she told herself proudly as she slid the letter
beneath the last on the stack without shedding a tear. She
could do this. She'd read a letter all the way through
without falling apart, and one that had the potential to
set her off on a crying jag. Confident that she had a
handle on her emotions, she pulled the next letter from
the stack.

Dearest Janine,
*We lost one of the guys in our unit yesterday.
North Vietcong were spotted in our area, and our*

unit was sent out to verify the report and to find out how many there were and how much firepower they packed. We'd been out two days without seeing any sign of the enemy and were ready to head back, when all hell broke loose.

We were near an old bomb crater and we made a run for it so we could form a defense and radio for a chopper. We managed to hold them off until aircraft could get there to give us cover from above. Just as we spotted the chopper coming in, somebody realized that Deek, one of the new guys in our unit, was missing.

We only had seconds to get into that chopper and get the hell out of there. There were still two of us on the ground—me and T.J.—when all of a sudden there was this sound like an Indian war whoop, followed by machine-gun fire. I glanced to my left and there was Deek, standing on the edge of that crater like he thought he was John Wayne, blasting away with his machine gun. I yelled for him to get down, but it was too late. The Vietcong had already spotted him.

He took the first hit in the neck, and that was probably what killed him. He took about twenty more before his body slid behind the rim of the crater and out of their sights. T.J. and I dragged him to the chopper and brought him back to base. I imagine his parents have gotten word by now. I just hope they never know that he was stoned out of his mind when he died.

Sometimes there's no satisfaction in saying "I told you so." That's the case with Deek. If he'd *listened to me and stayed clear of drugs, he might be alive today. Of course, he might've caught one anyway. That's the hell of it. You never know when your number is gonna come up.*

In some ways, I owe Deek my thanks. Watching him die changed my life. I was awake most of the night, thinking back over mistakes I've made in the past, and I've come up with a plan. In the future, I'm not going to be so slow about telling people what I think or how I feel about them. I'm going to be more open to new ideas and less judgmental of those I don't agree with. And I'm going to be quicker to forgive. You never know when you're going to run out of time to make things right.

I love you, Janine.
Larry

Stephanie lowered the letter and stared blindly at the wall, numbed by the vivid scene her father had described. She couldn't imagine what horrors he must have witnessed in Vietnam. Deek's death was probably only one of many he had witnessed during the eighteen months he'd spent overseas.

How did a person deal with that? she asked herself. What kind of emotional scars did it leave him with? And how did he ever sleep at night without being haunted by the memories?

She laid a hand over the page, thinking of the effect her father had claimed that Deek's death had had on his life. If he'd lived, what kind of man would he have been? she wondered. Certainly a wiser one, judging from the things he'd seen and the lessons he'd learned. Sadly he'd never had the chance to put into action his plan to improve his life even more.

Her eyes sharpened. But she could, she realized. She could take the things he'd planned to do and incorporate them into her own life. It would be a way of honoring her father, a way of giving his life purpose. It would be a means of making him a part of *her* life.

Wade stood in the doorway quietly watching Stephanie. She wasn't sobbing her heart out, which he considered a good sign. But she wasn't dancing a jig either. Her forehead was pleated, as if she were absorbed in some deep thought. And there were creases at the corners of her eyes and mouth, as if whatever she was thinking about was either sad or depressing.

"Did you finish reading the letters?"

She jumped, then placed a hand over her heart and released a long breath. "I didn't hear you come in."

Dragging off his hat, he stepped into the room. "Sorry. Next time I'll give a holler." He dropped down on the arm of the recliner. "So? How'd it go?"

Averting her gaze, she lifted a shoulder and drew the ribbon back around the stack of letters. "Okay, I guess. I only read two."

"Two?" he repeated and glanced at his watch. "They must've been long ones—I was gone almost an hour."

"Not long. Heavy."

"Oh," he said in understanding but offered nothing more. If she wanted to talk, he'd listen, but he wasn't going to force her to say anything she wasn't ready or willing to share.

Her expression growing pensive, she framed the stack of letters between her hands. "He was only twenty-one when he died," she said as if thinking aloud. "Yet he'd probably seen and experienced more than men twice his age."

"Yeah, I imagine he had."

She glanced up and met his gaze. "In the last letter I read, he wrote about a guy in his unit who was killed." Wincing, she shook her head. "It was awful just reading about it. I can't imagine what it must have been like to be there and witness it firsthand."

"War's no picnic. Ask any veteran."

Lowering her gaze, she plucked guiltily at the ribbon that bound the letters. "I'm ashamed to admit it, but most of my knowledge of war is purely historical. Dates, battles, the political ramifications. The kind of thing you learn in a classroom. And since I've never been a fan of war movies or novels, I've never had a visual to associate with it before." She shuddered. "And to be honest, I think I preferred it that way." She glanced up, her expression sheepish. "I guess that makes me sound like an ostrich, huh? Wanting to keep my head buried in the ground?"

Wade thought of his daughter and the current problems he was having with her and shook his head. "No. Innocence is a hard thing to hold on to in today's world. What with all the graphic and gruesome TV shows and movies being shown, I consider it a miracle that you've managed to hold on to even a smidgen of your innocence."

"Innocent? Me?" She choked back a laugh and shook her head. "I think I lost my innocence about the age of six, when Tammy Jones told me there was no Santa Claus."

He clapped a hand over his heart. "Please," he begged, "tell me it isn't so."

Hiding a smile, she set the bundle aside and drew her legs beneath her. "I didn't say there *wasn't* a Santa Claus. I was only repeating what Tammy told me."

He dragged an arm across his forehead in an exaggerated show of relief. "Whew. You scared me there for a minute. I'm counting on Santa bringing me the new Kubota tractor I've been lusting after."

"A tractor?" she repeated, then rolled her eyes. "Men and their toys."

"A tractor's not a toy," he informed her. "It's a machine."

She flapped a dismissing hand. "Whatever."

"Okay, Miss Smarty-Pants. What is Santa gonna bring you?"

She blinked as if startled by the question, then tears filled her eyes.

Wade swallowed a groan, realizing that with Bud gone, this would be her first Christmas alone—an actuality he'd just brutally reminded her of. Dropping to a knee, he covered her hand with his. "I'm sorry, Steph. I wasn't thinking."

Keeping her face down, she shook her head. "It's not your fault. I just…hadn't thought that far ahead."

Hearing the sadness in her voice and knowing he'd put it there made him feel about as low as a snake. In hopes of making it up to her, he caught her hand and pulled her to her feet. "Tell you what," he said. "As punishment for sticking my foot in my mouth, I'll give you an hour of slave labor. Haul boxes, carry out the garbage. You name it, I'm your man."

He sensed her resistance, but then she surprised him by giving her head a decided nod.

"All right," she said. "But remember, this was your idea, not mine."

Stephanie didn't know what had possessed her to accept Wade's backhanded offer of help...or maybe she did.

I'm going to be quicker to forgive. You never know when you're going to run out of time to make things right....

It was one of the ways her father had planned to change his life...and one of the changes Stephanie would have to make in her own if she was going to honor her father's memory by adopting his plan.

But could she forgive Wade? *Truly* forgive him?

She gave her head a shake as she placed the wrapped platter inside the box, unsure if that was possible.

"What pile does this go in?"

Pushing the hair back from her face, she looked up to see what Wade was holding. "Oh, wow," she murmured and reached to take the round of white plaster from him. "I haven't seen that in ages."

He hunkered down beside her. "What is it?"

"Don't you recognize fine art when you see it?" she asked, then smiled as she smoothed her hand across the shallow indentations in the plaster. "I made this in Bible school. Our teacher poured plaster in a pie pan, then had us press our hands into it to leave a print."

He placed his hand over the one impressed in the plaster. "Look how little that is," he said in amazement. "Mine is three or four times the size of yours."

She gave him a droll look. "I was five years old when I made that. I've grown some since then."

"Mine are still bigger." He held up his hand. "Put yours against mine," he challenged. "Let's see whose is bigger."

She hesitated slightly, reluctant to make the physical connection, then took a bracing breath and placed her palm against his. The warmth struck her first, followed by the strength she sensed beneath the flesh. She closed her eyes as awareness sizzled to life beneath her skin, from the top of her head to the tips of her toes.

"A good three inches longer," he boasted, pressing his fingers against hers. "Maybe more. And the breadth of my palm is at least two inches wider." He shifted his gaze to hers, then frowned and peered closer. "Steph? You okay? Your face is all red."

Of course it is, she wanted to tell him. Her body felt as if it were on fire and her mind was spinning, churning up memory after memory of what his hands could do to drive a woman out of her mind.

Dragging in a breath, she forced a smile. "Just a little dizzy. That's all." Flapping a dismissive hand, she laughed weakly. "I guess I've been pushing myself too hard to get all this done." She attempted to withdraw her hand, but he slid his fingers between hers, locking them together. Startled, she glanced up and met his gaze. In his eyes she saw the same awareness, the same need that burned behind her own. Unable to look away, she stared, slowly realizing that he was going to kiss her.

"Steph…"

At the last second she turned her face away and shook her head. "No. Don't. Please. I—"

"You what?"

Gulping back tears, she met his gaze. "I don't want you to kiss me. What happened before…I can't forget that."

She saw the anger that flashed in his eyes.

"Can't or won't?" he challenged.

Shaking her head, she dropped her gaze. "It doesn't matter. The result is the same."

He clamped his fingers down hard over her hand. "It may not matter to you, but it does to me. For God's sake, Steph! All that's in the past. Why can't you let it go?"

She snapped her gaze to his, furious that he would think it was that easy. "Because it hurts," she cried, fisting her free hand against her chest. "All these years later, and it still *hurts*."

He stared, the muscles in his face going slack. "You still care," he murmured, as if awed by the realization.

She shook her head wildly and tried to pull her hand free. "I don't. I *can't*."

He clamped his fingers tighter over hers, refusing to let her go. "You may not want to, but you can't deny what I see, what you feel."

A tear slipped past her lid and slid down her cheek.

"Aw, Steph," he said miserably. "I never meant to hurt you. That's the last thing I wanted to do. I asked then for your forgiveness and you refused." He dropped his gaze and shook his head. "Maybe that was asking too much of you. Could be it still is." He lifted his head to meet her gaze again, and she nearly wept at the regret that filled his eyes. "I know I destroyed whatever chance we ever had of being together, but couldn't we at least be friends?" He gave her hand a pleading squeeze. "Please, Steph? Is that too much to ask?"

She wanted desperately to tell him yes, it was too much to ask, to scream accusations and shoot arrows of blame until his heart was filled with as many holes as hers had been.

But she found she couldn't. And it was more than her desire to carry out her father's pledge of granting forgiveness that kept her from exacting her revenge. It was the pleading in his eyes and the sincerity in his voice that reached out and touched a place in her heart she'd thought could never be breached again.

But she wouldn't let him hurt her again. She couldn't. She would try her best to be his friend—but nothing more.

Drawing a steadying breath, she squared her shoulders. "I suppose we can try."

He stared a long moment, as if not trusting his ears, then dropped his chin to his chest and blew out a long breath. "Well, at least that's a start." Releasing her hand, he picked up the plaster disk of her handprint. "So what's it going to be? Trash, keep or donate?"

Grateful that he seemed willing to put the emotional scene behind them, she blinked to clear the tears from her eyes, then frowned as she studied the piece he held. Sagging her shoulders, she pointed to the pile marked Trash. "I'll probably hate myself later, but pitch it."

"If you want it, keep it."

Shaking her head, she picked up a china cup to wrap. "I'm already going to have to rent a storage facility as it is."

"But if it's special…" he argued.

"That's just it. Everything's special!" She placed the wrapped piece in the box, then waved a hand at the stuff piled around the room. "There isn't anything here that doesn't have a memory attached to it." She rocked to her knees and plucked a crystal bowl from the dining room table. "Take this, for instance. It belonged to my mother's mother. Mom told me that her mother always used it to serve her special fruit salad whenever they had company. Mom used it for the same thing. She even used the same fruit salad recipe her mother had always used." She opened a hand in a gesture of helplessness. "How do you throw away a piece of history like that?"

Wade picked up a piece of newspaper from the floor and handed it to her. "You don't. You either add on a room to your house or rent another storage building."

Stephanie frowned as he picked up another piece of paper and began to wrap it around the plaster handprint. "What are you doing? I told you to pitch that."

"A piece of art like this?" Shaking his head, he leaned to place it in the box with the china. "No way. That thing is priceless."

Tears filled her eyes as she watched him tuck the wrapped handprint into the box. It was such a simple thing, silly really, a kindness he was probably not even aware of. Yet his refusal to throw away a souvenir from her childhood put another crack in the armor she'd placed around her heart.

Fearing he'd do something else to widen the crack even more, she quickly wrapped paper around her grandmother's bowl. "What time is it?"

He glanced at his wristwatch. "One thirty-five."

She tucked the bowl into the box and stood, dusting off her hands. "Which means you've more than fulfilled your hour of slave labor."

"I can stay a little longer, if you want."

"Uh-uh." She turned him around and gave him a push toward the door. "Though I really appreciate all you did and hate losing the extra set of hands, I know darn good and well you've got work of your own to do."

"Yeah," he said, glancing at his wristwatch again. "I do."

At the door he stopped and looked back at her. "Steph, I'm glad we're going to be friends again."

She had to swallow back emotion before she could reply. "Yeah. Me, too."

Stephanie gave up and opened her eyes to stare at the dark ceiling. She'd tried everything to lull herself to sleep. She'd counted sheep, hummed the mantra from the yoga class she attended twice a week. She'd even gotten up and made herself a warm glass of milk to drink. Nothing had worked. Her mind still refused to shut down.

He would've kissed her. That one thought kept circling through her mind over and over again, keeping her awake. If she hadn't turned her face away, Wade would've kissed her. A part of her wanted to rail at the heavens that he would have the nerve to even try. Another part wished desperately that she had let him.

And that was what was keeping her awake. The fact that she still wanted his kiss. How pathetic. What woman in her right mind would knowingly and willingly subject herself to that kind of pain again?

Groaning, she dug her fingers through her hair as if she could tear thoughts of Wade from her mind. But that didn't help either. It just made her head ache even more.

Dropping her arms to her sides, she stared at the ceiling again, praying that sleep would come soon.

Runt growled, and she tensed, listening. Not hearing anything, she slowly dragged herself to a sitting position and leaned to peer at the rug beside the bed, where Runt slept.

"What is it, Runt?" she whispered. "Did you hear something?"

In answer, he rose and crossed to the door, the click of his nails on the wooden floor sounding like gunshots in the darkness.

Stephanie swung her legs over the side of the bed and hurried to stand beside the dog. "Is someone out there?" she whispered to Runt.

Whining low in his throat, he lifted a paw and scratched at the wood.

Though the dog couldn't see her face in the dark, she gave him a stern look. "If this is nothing more than you wanting to go outside to relieve yourself, I'm going to be really mad," she warned.

He barked once, sharply.

"Oh, Runt," she moaned, wringing her hands. "I really don't need this right now."

When he continued to whine and claw at the door, she gathered her courage and slowly opened the door a crack to peer out into the hall. Not seeing anything out of the ordinary, she opened the door wider. Runt pushed past her legs before she could stop him and shot down the hall, barking wildly. Stephanie's blood turned to ice as images of burglars and mass murderers filled her mind. Remembering the shotgun Bud kept behind the door in the laundry room, she crept down the dark hallway. As she passed through the kitchen, she whispered an impatient, "Give me a minute" to Runt, who was scratching at the back door and whining.

After locating the shotgun and checking to see that it was loaded and the safety was securely in place, she returned to the kitchen. She curled her fingers around the knob. "I'm right behind you," she murmured nervously to Runt, then opened the door.

The dog took off like a shot for the barn, his shrill bark sending shivers down her spine. She hesitated a second, trying to decide whether or not to grab a flashlight. Deciding that she couldn't shoot the gun and hold a flashlight, too, she ran after him.

A thick layer of storm clouds blanketed the sky, obliterating whatever illumination the moon might have offered. Stifling a shudder, Stephanie lifted the shotgun to her shoulder and moved stealthily toward the barn, keeping her finger poised on the trigger while keeping her ear cocked to the sound of Runt's barking.

A flash of lightning split the sky, making her jump, and was followed moments later by an earthshaking rumble of thunder. Silently vowing to murder Runt if this turned out to be a wild-goose chase, she quickened her step.

When she was about forty feet from the barn, Runt suddenly quit barking. Frowning, she strained, listening, but could hear nothing over the pounding of her heart. Tightening her grip on the shotgun, she flipped off the safety and tiptoed to the barn's dark opening.

Bracing a shoulder against the frame to steady her aim, she yelled, "Come out with your hands up!" in the deepest, meanest voice she could muster.

"Steph?"

She jolted at the sound of the male voice, then squinted her eyes against the darkness, trying to make out a shape. "Wade?" she asked incredulously. "Is that you?"

"Yeah, it's me."

The overhead lights flashed on and she squinted her eyes, momentarily blinded by the bright light. When her eyes adjusted, she saw Wade walking toward her. Runt trotted at his heels.

She didn't know whether to pull the trigger and shoot them both for scaring the daylights out of her or crumple into a heap of weak relief. Deciding murder was beyond her, she put the safety back on, lowered the shotgun and resorted to using her tongue as a weapon.

"What in blue blazes are you doing out here in the middle of the night?" she shouted at Wade. Before he could answer, she turned her fury on Runt. "And you," she accused angrily, "carrying on like burglars are crawling all over the place. You're supposed to protect me, not scare me to death. I have a good mind to take you to the *pound*."

Wade dropped a protective hand on the dog's head. "Don't blame Runt. It's my fault. I should've known he would hear me and kick up a fuss."

"Hear *what?*" she cried. "I was awake and I never heard a thing other than Runt barking." Realizing the oddity in that, she whipped her head around to look outside, then swung back around to face him. "Where's your truck?"

"At home. I walked."

"You *walked* all the way over here?"

He shoved his hands in his pockets and shrugged. "Couldn't sleep, so I figured I'd check on a heifer that's about to calf. She's young," he explained further, "and Bud was worried about her having trouble with the birth. I penned her when I was here earlier, so I could keep an eye on her."

"You walked," she repeated, unable to get beyond the incredibility in that one statement.

"It's not that far. Not if you cut through the woods."

She pressed the heel of her hand against her forehead and shook her head in disbelief. "I can't believe you did that. There's no telling what kind of varmints are hiding out in there."

He hid a smile. "I didn't run into a single grizzly or mountain lion."

She dropped her hand to frown. "Big surprise, since neither have been seen around here in fifty years or more. But there are coyotes and rattlesnakes," she reminded him, "and they can be just as dangerous."

When he merely looked at her, she rolled her eyes. "Men," she muttered under her breath. "If you cracked open the heads of the entire gender, you might come up with enough brains to form one good mind."

Lightning flashed behind her, followed by a deafening boom of thunder that made her jump.

Chuckling, he took the shotgun from her and caught her arm. "Come on," he said, tugging her along with him. "You better get back to the house before the bottom falls out of the sky."

She hurried to match her steps to his longer stride. "What about you? How will you get home?"

"The same way I came. I'll walk."

She dug in her heels, dragging him to a stop. "But you'll get soaked!"

He shrugged and nudged her into a walk again. "I've been wet before. I won't melt."

The words were no sooner out of his mouth, then the bottom of the sky did open up and rain poured down in torrents.

He grabbed her hand and shouted, "Run!"

Stephanie didn't need persuading. She took off, slipping and sliding on the wet grass, as Wade all but dragged her behind him. He reached the back door a step ahead of her and flung it open. Stephanie ducked inside and flipped on the light and was followed quickly by a drenched Runt. Wade brought up the rear, stripping off his hat and propping the gun against the wall before closing the door behind him.

"Man!" he exclaimed, dragging a sleeve across his face to swipe the rain from it. "That's some storm."

Stephanie grabbed a couple of dish towels from a drawer and tossed one to him before squatting down to rub a towel over Runt.

"Don't try to make up to me now," she scolded as Runt licked gratefully at her face. "If not for you and your stupid barking, we'd both be high and dry instead of dripping wet."

Wade hunkered down beside her and took the towel from her hand. "Here, let me. I'm the one to blame, not Runt."

Scowling, Stephanie stood and folded her arms across her breasts. "You won't get an argument out of me." A chill shook her, and she turned for the laundry room, where she'd left a basket of clean laundry. "I'm going to change clothes," she called over her shoulder.

She quickly stripped off her wet nightgown, dried off

as best she could with a towel she pulled from the basket, then tugged on a tank top and shorts. Grabbing one of her father's T-shirts from a stack on the dryer, she returned to the kitchen.

She offered the T-shirt to Wade. "It probably won't fit, but at least it's dry."

"Thanks." With a grateful smile he took the T-shirt and began to unbutton his shirt one-handed.

Stephanie didn't intend to watch but found she couldn't look away, as with each short drop of his hand to the next button, more and more of his chest was revealed. She knew from the summer they'd spent together, he often worked bare-chested. As a result, the skin he bared was as tanned as that on his face and hands, and the soft hair that curled around his nipples and rivered down to his navel had been bleached blonde.

By the time he reached the waist of his jeans and gave the shirt a tug, pulling his shirttail from beneath it, her mouth was dry as dust. Embarrassed by her reaction to such an innocent sight—and fearing he would notice his effect on her—she quickly turned away. As she did, the lights blinked out.

"Oh, great," she muttered. "Now the electricity is off."

"There's a candle on the shelf to the right of the sink."

Already on her way to fetch it, Stephanie shot him a frown over her shoulder. "I know where the candles are kept."

"Sorry."

As she struck a match and touched the flame to the wick, she frowned. The fire flickered a moment, then caught, tossing shadows to dance across the room.

Turning, she held the candle up and eyed Wade warily as he tugged Bud's T-shirt over his head. "How do you know so much about everything around here?"

He glanced up, then set his jaw and pulled the T-shirt down to his waist. "You may have shut me out of your life, but your parents didn't choose to do the same."

"You mean, you— They—"

"Yep, that's exactly what I mean." He stooped to pick up the towel he'd dried Runt with, then stood to face her. "Your mother was a little slower to forgive than Bud, but I think she finally realized I'd done the only thing an honorable man could've done in a situation like the one I was caught in."

Afraid she would drop it, Stephanie set the candle-holder on the table and pressed a hand to her stomach, suddenly feeling ill. "But they never said a word. Never so much as mentioned your name to me."

He tossed the wet towel into the sink. "That was out of respect for you, knowing it would upset you."

She dropped her face to her hands. "I can't believe this," she said. "How could they *do* that to me?"

"Oh, come on, Steph," he chided gently. "They didn't do anything to you." When she didn't respond, he crossed to pull her hands down, forcing her to look at him. "You know your parents loved you. They'd never do anything to hurt you."

"But they forgave you!" she cried. "Knowing what you had done to me, they still forgave you."

"One has nothing to do with the other," he argued.

When she opened her mouth to voice her disagreement, he silenced her with a look.

"They forgave me for what I'd done," he told her

firmly, "but not for the pain I caused you. I don't think they were ever able to forgive me for that."

She tossed up her hands. "What else was there to forgive?"

"Getting a woman pregnant and having to marry her."

Stunned, Stephanie stared, unable to believe that hearing him voice his transgression could have the same debilitating effect as it had when he'd confessed it to her so many years before.

Before she could cover her ears, refusing to hear any more, he caught her hands and held them, forcing her to hear him out.

"I never loved Angela. That's not something I'm proud of, considering, but it's true. I loved *you,* Steph, with all my heart and soul. Your parents knew that and knew, too, how much it cost me to lose you." He tightened his grip on her hands. "But don't hold their kindness to me against your mom and dad. Without them—" he dropped his chin to his chest and slowly shook his head "—I don't know how I would've survived it all."

Heaving a sigh, he gave her hands a last squeeze and turned away. "I guess I'd better go so you can get to bed." He stooped to give Runt's head a pat. "You might want to take a couple of candles with you to your bedroom," he said, the suggestion directed to Stephanie. "The electricity might not come back on until morning."

She watched him cross the kitchen, her throat squeezed so tight she could barely breathe.

I loved you, Steph, with all my heart and soul.

Out of everything he'd said, that one single statement filled her mind, obliterating all else.

He made it to the door before she found her voice. "I loved you, too."

His hand on the knob, he glanced back.

The tears clotting her throat rose to fill her eyes. "And you broke my heart."

Four

Wade stood, paralyzed as much by the desolation that etched Stephanie's face as by what she had just said. This was the woman he'd loved—still loved, if he was honest with himself—and, by her own admission, he'd broken her heart. He'd known he had—or at least had assumed that was the case—but it cut him to the bone to hear her say the words and see, this many years later, how much she still suffered from his infidelity.

He hadn't been able to comfort her then. How could he, when she wouldn't let him past her front door?

But he could now.

In two long strides he was across the room and had her face gathered between his hands. "I'm so sorry, Steph." He swept his thumbs beneath her eyes, swiping away the tears. "I never wanted to hurt you. I swear, if there'd been any other way…"

Realizing how inadequate the apology sounded, even to his own ears, he tightened his hands on her face, desperate to make her believe him. "You didn't deserve what I did to you. The sin was mine. You had no part in it, yet you paid a price." He swallowed hard. "But I paid, too, Steph. If you want the truth, I'm still paying."

He saw the flash of surprise in her eyes, the hope that rose slowly to glimmer in the moisture.

Helpless to do anything less, he lowered his face and touched his lips to hers. It wasn't a passionate kiss. A mere meeting of lips. But to Wade it was like coming home after a long stay away. He withdrew far enough to draw a shuddery breath, then wrapped his arms around her and pressed his mouth more fully over hers. He felt the shiver that trembled through her, swallowed the low moan that slid past her lips. With a groan he clamped his arms around her and opened his mouth over hers.

Her taste rushed through him like a swollen river, flooding him with memory after memory that he'd struggled for years to forget. The feel of her lying naked in his arms, the almost greedy race of her hands over his flesh. Her catlike purr of pleasure vibrating against his chest, the moist warmth of her laughter teasing his chin.

Rock-hard and wanting more of her, he hooked a hand beneath her knee, lifted and drew her hard against his groin. But it wasn't enough. Not nearly enough. With his mouth locked to hers, he backed her up against the wall and leaned into her, pinning her there with his body. Filling his hands with her rain-dampened hair, he held her face to his and took the kiss deeper still, until his breath burned in his lungs and his veins pumped liquid fire, until every cell in his body throbbed with his need to take her, to make her his again.

Bracing his hand in a V at her throat, he dragged his lips from hers. "I want you, Steph," he whispered and rained kisses over her face, her eyelids, across the hollows of her cheeks. "I want to make love with you." He pushed a knee between her legs and buried his face in the curve of her neck to smother a groan as her heat burned through his thigh.

Though he knew her need equaled his, he sensed her hesitancy in the tremble of hands she braced against his chest and feared he was pushing her too fast, too hard.

Drawing in a long breath to steady himself, he dragged his hand from her throat to cover her breast. Beneath his palm he could feel the pounding of her heart.

"Remember how good we were together?" Closing his fingers around her fullness, he gently kneaded. "I always loved your breasts." He lifted the one he held and warmed it with his breath. Humming his pleasure when her nipple budded beneath the thin fabric, he flicked his tongue over the swollen peak.

She arched instinctively, thrusting her breast against his mouth. He nipped, suckled, nipped again, but quickly became frustrated by the fabric that kept him from fully touching her, tasting her. "I want you bare," he said, then looked up at her, seeking her permission.

She gulped, nodded, then dropped her head back against the wall on a low moan as he eased her tank top down far enough to expose her breast. The candle behind him tossed light to flicker over her flushed flesh— the knotted bud, the pebbled areola that surrounded it, the lighter skin stained with the blush of desire. Mesmerized by the sight, he opened his mouth over her nipple, drew her in.

As he suckled, teasing her nipple with his tongue and teeth, he sensed her growing need in the hands she gripped at his head, her impatience in the fingers she knotted in his hair. Anxious to satisfy both, he released her and swept her up into his arms.

Leaving the candle behind in the kitchen, he made his way through the dark house, his familiarity with her parents' home guiding his steps. Once inside her bedroom, he pushed the door shut with his foot, in case Runt decided to follow, and continued on to her bed. He laid her down, then stretched out alongside her.

In the darkness he couldn't see her face, didn't need to in order to know that somewhere along the short walk from the kitchen to her bedroom her hesitancy had returned. He could all but feel the years that lay between them, all the days and months, stacked one on top of the other, in which she had clung to her resentment toward him, shored up a wall around her heart that he had only just begun to believe he could tear down. He had the power to seduce her. He knew that. He'd proven it in the kitchen only moments before. But he couldn't allow his physical needs to destroy whatever chance he might still have with her.

Placing a hand on her cheek, he turned her face to his. "You'll never know how much I've missed you," he said softly. "How many nights I've dreamed of touching you and holding you like this." He drew in a deep breath, anxious to make her understand how he truly felt. "But it's so much more than the sex. I've missed *you*, Steph. Your laughter, your smile. The way you always seemed to know exactly what I needed, whether it was a swift quick in the seat of the pants or a tight hug of encouragement. The hours we spent talking. And the times we spent in silence, content just to be together."

He caught her hand and drew it to his lips. "I'd be lying if I said I didn't want you right now. But more than the sexual release and pleasure that would give me—hopefully both of us—I need *you*. Back in my life, back in my heart. When we make love again, Steph, I want you to want me as much as I want you. I don't want there to be any regrets."

He heard her breath hitch and he swept his thumb across her cheek to catch the tear that fell. "Don't cry, Steph." He slipped his arm beneath her and drew her to him, tucking her head beneath his chin. "Just let me hold you. That's all I'll do, I swear, is just hold you."

Steph awakened and stretched her legs out, while wisps of sensations and emotions floated through her mind. Her eyes still closed, she separated each, naming them. Warmth. Tenderness. Comfort. Security. Lust. She stiffened at the latter and tried to remember if she'd had a dream that would explain why she'd wake with that particular thought on her mind.

Wade, she realized slowly as the events of the previous night returned. He'd aroused her with his seductive words, his lips, his touch. Even as she remembered the way his mouth had felt on her breast, the tremble of desire he'd drawn, she had to squeeze her thighs tight against the ache that throbbed to life deep in her womb.

She remembered, too, the trepidation that had grown inside her with each step he'd taken that had brought them closer to her bedroom. *Distrust.* It was such an ugly and debilitating word, one that she had lived with for far too many years. But as hard as she'd tried to banish it from her mind, it was always there in her subconscious, keeping her from giving her heart to any man—even, it seemed, the one responsible for planting the seed inside her in the first place.

But he'd claimed that he had suffered as much as she. And, if he was to be believed, he was still suffering. Remembering how he'd pulled her into his arms, telling her that he wanted only to hold her, she closed her eyes and gave herself up to the warmth and sense of security she'd found there.

Stiffening, she flipped her eyes open, suddenly wide-awake. Was he still here with her? she wondered. In her bed? Holding her breath, she dropped a hand behind her and groped. When her fingers met only cool sheets, she slowly brought her hand back to curl beneath her cheek, swallowing back the disappointment at finding him gone.

And why would you be sad about that? she asked herself. You should be relieved that he left. You don't need this, she reminded herself. You've got enough drama going on in your life without adding Wade to the mix.

With a sigh she flipped back the covers, preparing to get up, but froze when a piece of paper fluttered up from the pillow next to hers and drifted slowly out of sight on the far side of the bed. Making a dive for it, she flattened her stomach against the mattress and caught it before it hit the floor. Her heart in her throat, she sat up, bracing her back against the headboard and read.

*Good morning, Sunshine. Sorry to leave without
waking you, but you were sleeping so soundly I
hated to disturb you, figuring you needed the rest.
I'll be back around noon to drop off another
bundle of letters. If you want, after I check on the
cattle, I can stay for a while and help you pack.
Wade*

She shifted her gaze to read the first line again, and
a warm glow slowly spread through her chest. *Sunshine.*
It was a nickname he'd used often the summer they'd
met. Surprised that he would remember the endearment,
she sank back against her pillow and stared out the
window, her thoughts growing pensive as she wondered
where all this was going.

Judging by the passionate scene in the kitchen the
previous night, she had to believe that he was hoping
they could be more than friends.

But she wasn't sure she could offer him anything
more than friendship. He'd destroyed her trust, hurt her
more than words could ever describe. How did a person
get over that kind of pain, humiliation? Was it even
possible? Forgiving was one thing, forgetting another.
And if she couldn't forget, what was the point in getting
involved with him again? Even if she were willing to
agree to a strictly physical relationship, the past would
always be there between them.

She shivered, remembering the way his mouth had
felt on her breast, the desperate need that had burned
through her body, leaving her weak and wanting. He
had been right in saying that they'd been good together.
They *had* been good together—though she had to give

all the credit to Wade. She'd yet to meet the man who could satisfy her the way he once had. He had always seemed to understand her needs better than she did herself, knowing what pleased her, the areas of her body that were most sensitive, when she craved speed and when she preferred a slow seduction…and when she needed him to stop altogether.

He'd recognized the latter the previous night. Without her having to say a word, he'd somehow known that at some point between the kitchen and bedroom the ugly doubts had arisen, making her question what they were doing and whether or not she should allow things to go any further. Before she had even reached a decision, he'd removed her need to do so by voicing her fears aloud and refusing to make love with her until she could do so without regret.

She drew in a shuddery breath and slowly released it. How in the heck was a woman supposed to deal with a man like that? she asked herself. One who knew her fears as well as she did, then offered her his understanding and patience while she dealt with them?

Hearing Steph's faint call of, "The door's open," Wade stepped inside.

"I'm back here!"

Since her voice was coming from the rear of the house, he assumed by "here" she meant one of the bedrooms. Taking the shortcut through the dining room, he glanced around and was surprised to find the table was clear and all the boxes were stacked neatly against one wall.

He stuck his head into the guest room and found

her standing on a ladder inside the closet, her head hidden from view. She was wearing shorts, and the view of her long, tanned legs and bare feet put a knot of need in his groin. Puffing his cheeks, he blew out a long breath to steady himself, then tossed the bundle of letters onto the bed. "Looks like you've been busy."

"And then some," came her weary reply. She backed down the ladder, balancing a stack of shoe boxes on the palm of one hand. Reaching the floor, she steadied the stack with her opposite hand and stooped to set them on the floor. Straightening, she blew a breath at the wisps of hair that had escaped the ponytail she'd pulled her hair into, then smiled. "But I'm making progress. I finished the dining room and now I'm working in here."

He looked around at the piles that covered the floor, amazed by the amount of junk she'd unearthed. "Where did all this stuff come from?"

She hooked her thumb over her shoulder at the closet. "In there. Can you believe Mom was able to cram all that junk in that small a space?"

He picked up a doll that lay on the foot of the bed. A black hole gleamed from the space where an eye should have been, and blond hair frizzed from its scalp. He lifted a brow. "Yours?"

Smiling fondly, she took the doll from him. "This is Maddy. I wagged her around from the age of three to about seven or eight, I think."

"What happened to her eye?"

"One of Bud's dogs got a hold of her and popped it out."

"The dog get her hair, too?"

She shook her head and attempted to smooth the

wild tufts. "No, that was my doing. I thought she'd look better with a short hairstyle."

He sat down on the edge of the bed. "Remind me to never get near you when you've got a pair of scissors in your hand."

Chuckling, she laid the doll on the dresser. "Coward."

In her reflection in the dresser mirror he watched her smile slowly fade and knew by the creases that appeared between her brows that something was bothering her.

"About last night," she began uneasily.

Not wanting to have that particular discussion with her halfway across the room, he stretched to catch her hand and tugged her over to sit down beside him. "What about last night?"

She glanced at him, then away, her cheeks flaming a bright red. "I'm sure that you must think I'm giving off…"

When her voice trailed off, he bit back a smile. "Mixed signals?" he suggested.

She looked at him, then dropped her chin and nodded. "One minute I'm stiff-arming you and the next I'm, well, I'm—"

"Melting into a puddle of rapturous joy at my feet?"

She shot him a frown. "I wouldn't go so far as to say *that*."

Chuckling, he slung an arm around her shoulders and hugged her to his side. "No need to get your panties in a twist. I was just trying to make you laugh so you'd relax a little."

She shot to her feet to pace. "That's the problem. It's way too easy to relax around you. So much so that I'm letting my guard down."

"And that's a bad thing?"

She whirled to face him. "Yes, it's a bad thing! You hurt me, and I can't forget that."

"But you've forgiven me."

It was a statement, not a question, and she stared, realizing it was true. She didn't know exactly when or even why, but she *had* forgiven him.

But what was the use of forgiving if she couldn't forget? she found herself thinking again.

"Give yourself time," he suggested as if he'd read her thoughts. "And me, too," he added. He caught her hand and tugged her to stand between his legs. "I'm going to win back your trust," he told her in a tone that left little doubt that he would succeed. Holding her gaze, he brought her hand to his lips and pressed a kiss to her knuckles. "The burden is mine to prove, not yours."

She blinked back tears at the depth of his determination, the tenderness with which he'd made the promise to win back her trust. Yet she couldn't help questioning her sanity for her willingness to breathe so much as the same air as him after what he'd done to her.

Again as if reading her mind, he took her hands in his. "I'm not perfect, Steph. I've made my share of mistakes. But loving you was never one of 'em."

Her face crumpling, she sank to his knee and dropped her forehead against his. "Oh, Wade," she said miserably. "Why does everything have to be so complicated?"

He turned her face up to his. "It doesn't have to be. At least, not the part that deals with us. We were good together, good for each other. And we will be again."

She lifted her head to search his eyes and knew by the warmth she found there that he was offering her a new beginning, one that she was finding difficult to refuse. He made it sound so simple, so easy. But was it really?

"Wade—"

He touched his lips to hers to silence her. "You don't need to say anything. I'm not pushing for something you're not ready to give."

She closed her eyes, gulped. When she opened them and met his gaze, saw the warmth and understanding there, what little hesitancy that remained to hold her back slipped soundlessly away.

She lifted a hand to his cheek, her fingers trembling as she traced the lines that fanned from the corner of his eye. "You don't have to push. I'm more than ready."

He stared, as if not trusting his ears. "Are you sure?"

"Yes," she murmured and touched her lips to his.

Groaning, he wrapped his arms around her and pulled her to his chest. With an urgency that left her head spinning and her heart racing, he stripped off her blouse, her bra, then twisted her around on his lap and fitted her knees on either side of his thighs.

"Sweet heaven," he murmured as his gaze settled on her breasts. He filled his hands with their softness. "So beautiful." Sweeping his hands around to settle beneath them, he lifted and placed a kiss on each peak. He tipped up his head to meet her gaze and stroked his thumbs over her nipples. "Exactly as I remember them, perfect in every way."

Knowing it wasn't true, she shook her head. "You're a wonderful liar, but age and gravity have taken their toll."

"Perfect," he insisted, then teased her with a smile. "I think I'm the better judge."

She tipped her head, willing to concede the point,

then gasped as he closed his mouth over a nipple. Dropping her head back, she clung to his head. "Wade," she said, his name rushing out on thready sigh, then gasped again as he caught the nipple between his teeth and tugged gently. "Oh, Wade," she groaned and knotted her fingers in his hair.

Desperate to have her hands on him, she reached for his shirt and fumbled open buttons. Halfway down, she grew impatient and shoved the plackets apart and sank against him to press her lips against the middle of his chest. She inhaled once, released it with a contented sigh, then inhaled again and held the breath, absorbing his male scent.

Dizzy from it, she braced her hands against his chest and began a slow journey of exploration, smoothing her palms over the swell of muscled chest, down, her fingers bumping over each rib, then bringing her hands together at the waist of his jeans. Finding the snap, she released it and eased the zipper down.

With her lungs burning for air, her chest heaving with her attempts to fill them, she found his mouth with hers and freed his sex. It sprang from the restraining clothing and filled her hands. Marveling at the feel of silk-sheathed steel, she stroked her fingers down its length until the heel of her hand bumped the nest of coarse hair at its base. She released a shuddery breath against his lips and stroked upward, gathering her fingers at its tip and swirling her thumb over the pearl of moisture there.

With a groan he fell back, bringing her with him, and toed off his boots, his socks, then, one-handed, stripped off his jeans and underwear. Letting his clothing fall to the floor, he dragged her up his body and captured her mouth again. He kissed her with an urgency that fed her own need, yet with a tenderness that twisted her heart.

Noonday sun shone through the windows at either side of the bed, filling the room with bright sunlight. Though she would've preferred candlelight to mask the changes age had left on her body, Stephanie was grateful for the illumination, as it provided her the ability to see Wade's face, the muscled lines of his body her hands traced. With each glide of flesh over flesh, the years fell away, leaving in their place the familiarity she'd once known with this man, the ease they'd once shared.

Desperate to have him inside her again, to experience the thrill of oneness she'd once known, she wiggled out of her shorts and panties, then positioned her knees on either side of his hips. Using her hand to guide him, she dragged his sex along her folds to moisten it, then positioned the tip at her opening. With her gaze on his, she drew in a deep breath, bracing herself, then plunged her hips down and took him in.

The sensations that ripped through her stole her breath and sent brilliant shards of white to explode behind her closed lids. His name became a fervent prayer for release she whispered as she pumped her hips against his. Again and again and again, until sweat beaded her upper lip, slicked her hands, making it all but impossible to keep them braced against his chest. The pressure built inside her, fed by a rising wave of need that gathered itself into a knot in her womb.

As if sensing her readiness, her need for satisfaction, Wade clamped his hands at her hips. "Come with me," he said breathlessly, then set his jaw and squeezed his eyes shut. A low growl rose from deep inside him, then he exploded inside her, and the heat that pulsed from him sent her soaring high.

Her lungs heaving like bellows, her hands fisted against his chest, she hovered a moment, suspended on that needlelike peak of pain and pleasure, wanting more than anything to hold on in order to capture the feelings and emotions that filled her. Unable to stave off the sensations any longer, she toppled over the other side into satisfaction.

Weak, sated, she sank to his chest and buried her face in the curve of his neck, every nerve in her body quivering liked plucked strings. "Oh, Wade," she whispered, unable to find the words to express the experience.

"Was it good?"

Inhaling, she stretched her toes out and curled her feet around his sweat-dampened calves. "Oh, yeah," she said, releasing the breath on a contented sigh. "Better than good."

Before she had time to draw another breath, she was on her back and he was on top of her, his face only inches from her.

"Honey, that was nothing but foreplay. What comes next ranks right up there with fantastic."

Laughing, she laced her fingers behind his neck and brought his face down to hers. "Then show me what you've got, cowboy."

Five

The next day Wade was in his toolshed early, anxious to get his work done so that he could go and see Steph.

After selecting a wrench from those hanging on the wall above his worktable, he hunkered down in front of the baler to adjust the belt's tension. He had made only two full turns when the wrench slipped and he had to stop and swipe the perspiration from his hands—and it wasn't the heat that had made his hands slick with sweat, although his toolshed held heat like a smokehouse. It was the thoughts of Steph that kept playing through his mind.

Aware of the dangers involved in working on a piece of equipment and knowing how much they escalated if a man wasn't giving his full attention to the job, he pulled the wrench free and braced it against his thigh. He still couldn't believe they'd made love. He'd hoped they would, planned on it even, but he'd thought it would take him a lot longer to persuade her.

He didn't know what had changed her mind and really didn't care. The only thing that mattered was that she'd given herself to him willingly and without any pressure from him. Not that he would have felt any compunction on applying a little, if she'd dragged her feet too much longer. From the moment he'd seen her standing in her parents' house a week ago he'd known that his feelings for her hadn't changed. Just looking at her had had the same debilitating effect on him that it had thirteen years before. And kissing her…well, he wouldn't even go there, seeing as he couldn't even hold on to a wrench, as it was.

"Dad-dy! I'm talking to you!"

Wade glanced over to find his daughter standing in the doorway, her hands fisted on her hips. Setting the wrench aside, he dragged a rag from his pocket to wipe his hands. "Sorry, sweet cheeks. Guess I was daydreaming. Whatcha need?"

She pushed her hands into fists at her sides, with an impatient huff of breath. "I *asked* if I could spend the night with Brooke."

Eyeing his daughter warily, he stuffed the rag back into his pocket, wondering whether this overnight was on the up-and-up or a smoke screen she was spreading for her to do God only knew what. "Did Brooke's mother say it was all right with her?"

She gave him a pained look, one she'd perfected over the last year, then said through clenched teeth, "Yes. She said I could ride the bus home with Brooke after school if it's okay with you."

Knowing from experience that this could all be a clever lie Meghan was weaving in order to cover her tracks, he pulled his cell from the holster at his waist. "I'll just give Jan a call and double-check things with her."

"Daddy!" she cried. "I told you Mrs. Becker said it was okay!"

He punched in the number, then looked down his nose at her as he lifted the phone to his ear. "If it's all the same to you, I'd like to hear that from Jan."

She folded her arms across her chest and pushed her lips out in a pout. "You don't trust me."

He listened through the second ring. "The last time you asked permission to go somewhere with a girl-friend, you ended up at the pizza parlor with a guy two years older than you." When she opened her mouth to spew a comeback, he held up a hand, silencing her.

"Jan?" he said into the receiver. "This is Wade Parker, Meghan's dad."

He listened a moment, then smiled. "Doing just fine. How about yourself?"

"That's good," he replied to her response that all was well in the Becker household, then scratched his head. "Listen, Jan. Meghan was telling me about her plans to spend the night with Brooke tonight, and I wanted to make sure that was all right with you before I gave her my permission."

He listened again, then breathed a sigh of relief at her affirmative answer. "No, riding the bus home with Brooke is fine with me," he told her. "Will save you and me both from having to haul them around."

He smiled and nodded again. "Yeah, I hear you. These girls would keep us in the middle of the road if they could." Anxious to end the call before Jan got started in on the trials and tribulations of being a single parent, he said, "I'd better go. I need to write a permission note for Meghan to give the bus driver before she leaves for school." He nodded again. "You, too, Jan. And thanks."

He disconnected the call and returned his cell to its holster.

Meghan lifted a haughty brow. "Well? Are you satisfied *now?*"

Wade pulled a tablet from a slot above his worktable and scrawled a note granting his permission for Meghan to ride a different bus from school. "Better watch your mouth, young lady, or you'll find yourself spending the night at home with me."

She snatched the note from his hand and spun for the house. "And wouldn't that be fun?" she muttered under her breath.

Wade heard the sassy comeback but chose to ignore it. He'd learned the hard way to choose his battles with his daughter, and this one wasn't even worth the energy required for a skirmish.

Heaving a sigh, he braced a hand on the doorjamb and watched her stalk to the house, her long blond hair swinging from side to side with each angry stride. Twelve going on twenty-two, he thought sadly. Why couldn't kids just be satisfied with being kids? he asked himself. Why were they so hell-bent on becoming adults? Didn't they realize that being a grown-up wasn't all it was cracked up to be? Kids didn't have the responsibilities and worries that adults faced every day. Hell, this was the best time of Meghan's life! She should be enjoying herself, instead of plotting and scheming ways to do things she wasn't allowed to do. Things that she was too *young* to be doing.

He shook his head, remembering the day she'd come home sporting three holes in each ear and knowing it was too late for him to do a damn thing to stop her from doing it. And what was with this new infatuation of hers with boys two and three years older than herself?

Snorting, he dropped his hand from the door and turned back to the baler he'd been working on. He may not know what his daughter was thinking, but he knew what was on those boys' minds. And that was the problem. It wasn't so long ago that he'd been a teenage boy that he couldn't recognize a hormone-raging stud looking for a girl he could charm out of her panties when he saw one.

He shuddered at the thought of his daughter being sexually active, then set his jaw and picked up his wrench, settling it into place over a bolt. "Not on my watch," he muttered and gave the wrench a hard turn, tightening the bolt into place.

Stephanie opened the door and blinked in surprise when she saw Wade standing on the stoop, his hat in his hand. "What are you doing over here at this time of day?"

His smile sheepish, he scuffed the toe of his boot at the doormat. "I'm embarrassed to admit to being this slow, but it only just occurred to me that it's Friday night and I've got nothing to do. I thought, if you weren't busy, we might go to a movie or something."

Stephanie would've laughed if he hadn't looked so

cute standing there like a lost puppy in search of a new home. She glanced down at her bare feet and the cutoff jeans she was wearing, then at her wristwatch. Wrinkling her nose, she shifted her gaze back to his. "By the time I shower and change, whatever movie is showing would be half over."

He grimaced. "Yeah, you're probably right. I should've called first. I started to, but I figured you wouldn't answer the phone."

"I wouldn't have." Taking pity on him, she opened the door wide. "Tell you what. We can watch a movie here. If there's nothing on, I'm sure I can find a video or DVD in my parents' stash for us to watch."

"Are you sure?" he asked even as he stepped eagerly inside. "If you're busy or have other plans, I can head back home. I'm sure I can find something there to do to pass the time."

Laughing, she closed the door behind him. "I'm not busy. In fact, I was just about to put a frozen pizza in the oven. Have you had dinner yet?"

He placed a hand over his stomach, as if only now realizing he'd missed the meal and was hungry. "No, as a matter of fact, I haven't."

She glanced at him over her shoulder as she led the way to kitchen. "Is pepperoni okay?"

He tossed his hat onto the counter. "Beggars can't be choosers."

She stopped, balancing a pizza on the palm of one hand, the other curled around the handle of the oven door. "If you don't like pepperoni, I can probably scrape up the makings for a sandwich."

Chuckling, he shook his head. "Pepperoni's fine. In

fact, that's all I ever eat. It's Meghan's favorite and the only one we keep stocked in our freezer."

Stephanie's smile faded.

Wade noticed the sudden change in her expression before she turned to slide the pizza into the oven and cursed his blunder, knowing it was his mention of his daughter that had robbed her of her smile. He crossed to her and caught her hand in his. "Steph, she's my daughter. I can't pretend she doesn't exist."

She squared her shoulders and forced a smile. "I know that. And I don't expect you to pretend she doesn't exist. You just—well, you caught me off guard when you mentioned her. You having a child is not something that I care to think about."

"But…" He stopped, knowing that anything else he said would only drag up more of the past. And he didn't want to spoil the one evening he had with her rehashing his mistakes.

"How about some wine?" he asked, changing the subject. "Bud usually kept a bottle or two around, if you haven't thrown them out."

She stepped around him and gestured to the far cabinet as she headed for the sink. "Up there, and the opener is in—" She stopped, hauled in a breath, then continued on to the sink. "Well, I'm sure you probably know where to find the opener, the same as you do the wine, since you seem to know where everything else is kept."

In two long strides he was across the room and turning her around to face him. His anger melted when he saw the gleam of tears in her eyes. "Aw, Steph," he said miserably. "I thought we'd already cleared that hurdle. Yes, I was friends with your parents. And yes, I know my way around their house probably as well as I do my own. But don't let that come between us. We've got enough old baggage to sort through without having to dredge up that particular subject again."

When she kept her head down, refusing to look at him, he hooked a finger beneath her chin and tipped her face up to his. "Come on, Steph. I know you feel like we all conspired against you, but that wasn't the case at all. Your parents knew that mentioning my name in any form or fashion would only upset you, so they didn't."

She closed her hand over his and drew in a breath. "I know. And I'm sorry. Really. It's just going to take time for me to get used to…well, everything. So much went on that I wasn't aware of." She held up a hand when he started to interrupt. "Which is my fault," she said, saving him from having to tell her it was. Drawing his hand to hold between hers, she gave it a reassuring squeeze. "Now about that wine…"

He dropped a kiss on her mouth. "Frozen pizza and wine. Is there something wrong with this picture?"

"I'd say it's right on par with every date I ever had with you."

"Hey!" he cried, looking insulted. "We went on a couple of real dates."

She folded her arms across her chest. "Name one."

He shifted from one foot to the other, trying to think of one to offer, then gave her a sheepish look. "I guess I did kind of drop the ball in the date department."

Laughing, she patted his cheek. "No, you didn't. I always enjoyed the time we spent together, no matter what we were doing."

Relieved that it appeared they had weathered another

storm, he pulled out a drawer and drew out the wine opener. "Remember the time you sat up all night with me when my mare was foaling?"

"Yes. That was the first equine birth I'd ever witnessed. And hopefully my last," she added with a shudder. "That poor mare. It was hard to watch her suffer when there was nothing we could do to ease her pain."

"Breach births are seldom easy," he said as he pulled the cork from the bottle with a *pop*. "I've probably lost as many babies as I've saved. Sometimes lost the mamas, too."

While he filled two wineglasses, Stephanie set the timer on the oven. "That's the one thing I don't miss about living on a ranch," she said thoughtfully as she crossed to stand beside him. "Losing an animal always made me so sad."

"Yeah, it does me, too." He handed her a glass, then draped an arm along her shoulders. "Want to sit on the patio while we wait for the pizza to cook?"

"Good idea."

Once outside, she brushed a hand over the seats of the chairs, sweeping away the dried leaves that covered them, then sat and patted the chair next to hers. "Take a load off."

He nudged the chair closer to hers, then dropped down with a sigh.

"I love this view," she said, her smile wistful as she stared out at the pastures and the low hills beyond. "The way the sun looks at sunset, as if it's melting into the hills."

He laced his fingers through hers and settled their joined hands on the arms of their pushed-together chairs. "It is pretty. I have almost this exact same view from the balcony off my bedroom."

Her gaze still on the setting sun, she hid a smile. "I remember both the balcony and the view." She waited a beat, then added, "I also remember you spreading a blanket on the balcony one night and getting me drunk on tequila shots."

He pressed a hand against his chest. "Me?" He shook his head. "You must be mistaken. I'd never take advantage of a woman that way."

She bumped her shoulder against his. "Oh, please. And that wasn't the only time you got me drunk. I distinctly remember a case of beer and an afternoon spent skinny-dipping in the creek that runs through your hay field."

"It was hot," he said defensively. "And as I recall, you only had two of those beers."

She lifted a shoulder. "What can I say? I'm a cheap drunk."

Biting back a smile, he tapped his glass against hers. "Drink up, then. Maybe I'll get lucky again tonight."

She drew back to look at him in surprise. "How long are you planning to stay?"

"All night, if you'll let me."

She dropped her mouth open, then slowly closed it to stare. "You mean…you can stay the whole night?"

He took her glass and set it, along with his, on the patio. "Yep," he said and tugged her from her chair and onto his lap. "The *whole* night."

She continued to stare, realizing the significance in that. "Do you realize this will be the first time we will have ever slept together?"

He grasped her thigh and shifted her more comfortably on his lap. "I think you're forgetting about the night it stormed."

"No. That doesn't count because you were gone when I woke up."

He lifted a hand to her cheek and met her gaze squarely. "This one might not count either, because I'm not planning on either one of us getting any sleep."

The heat in his blue eyes burned through hers, turning her mouth to cotton and twisting her stomach into a pretzel.

The timer on the oven went off, its loud buzz signaling the pizza was done.

Unable to tear her gaze from his, she wet her lips. "Are you hungry?"

He hooked a hand behind her neck and brought her face to his. "Only for you," he said before closing his mouth over hers.

Her breath stolen, Stephanie wrapped her arms around him and clung. She felt as if she were drowning, slipping deeper and deeper into a sea of desire, its waters at first tinted a soft, muted blue, cocooning her as she drifted down. Then the water changed, became a fiery-red tempest that churned, battering her senses. The heat it produced gathered into a tight knot in her middle, then slowly spread out to every extremity, making her skin steam and her lungs burn for air.

"Wade," she gasped, remembering their dinner. "The pizza."

He slid a hand beneath her shirt, cupping a breast, and found her mouth again. "Let it burn."

Though tempted, she pushed a hand against his chest, forcing him back. "We can't. The house could burn, too."

Frowning, he pulled his hand from beneath her shirt.

"Okay, so we'll take the damn thing out." He stood, hitching her up high on his chest, and carried her back to the kitchen. "You do the honors."

With one hand locked around his neck to keep from falling, she plucked a mitt from the rack on the oven's front panel, then opened the door and pulled out the pizza. Wade angled her toward the range so that she could shove the pizza onto its flat surface.

He lifted a brow. "Satisfied?"

Locking her hands behind his neck, she gave him a coy look. "Not yet, but I'm counting on you taking care of that little problem for me."

He choked on a laugh, then turned for the door, his long ground-eating stride covering the distance between the kitchen and her bedroom in record time. Once in her room, he dumped her on her bed, then dived in after her. Hooking an arm over her waist, he rolled to his back and pulled her on top of him.

Smiling, he combed his fingers through her hair to hold it back from her face. "Now let's see what we can do about satisfying you."

"Don't you think we should get rid of some clothing first?"

He dragged his hands down her back and pushed them beneath the waistband of her shorts. "Eventually."

With the cheeks of her buttocks gripped firmly within his broad hands, he lifted his head and claimed her mouth. Stephanie surrendered with a delicious shiver, willing to follow wherever he led.

The path he chose for them was a wild one. At times treacherously steep, while at others lazy and meandering. At some point during their journey—she couldn't

remember when or how exactly—"eventually" occurred, and he peeled off their clothing, letting the
pieces fall where they may. While he explored her body,
she explored his, marveling at the muscles that swelled
and ebbed beneath her curious palms, the thunderous
beat of his heart against her lips, the soft pelt of light
blond hair that shot down his middle to the darker nest
between his legs.

Sure that no other man knew her as well as Wade,
nor could please her in so many fascinating and breath-
taking ways, she gave herself up to him, to them, to the
moment. She refused to think about the yesterdays in
their lives or the worries that tomorrow might bring. She
focused only on *now*.

And when he entered her, joining his body with hers,
she squeezed back the tears of joy that sprang to her
eyes at the sense of oneness that swept over her, the
sense of rightness in being here at this moment and in
this place with this man.

And when he'd given her the satisfaction he'd promised—and hopefully received an equal measure for himself—she curled naked against his side, laced her
fingers through his over his heart and slept.

Stephanie decided that sleeping with Wade was
almost as satisfying as making love with him. Cradled
like two spoons, her back to his front, her buttocks
nudged into the bowl shaped by his groin and thighs was
truly a heavenly experience. Adding to the pleasure was
having his knee wedged between hers and his arm
draped over her waist, keeping her snugged close. It
wasn't a position that either of them had choreographed

or maneuvered into after a lot of fidgeting and adjusting. It had just…happened. Naturally.

And that made her smile.

She knew couples who struggled for years to find the perfect sleeping arrangement. Others who were still struggling. Yet she and Wade had slid naturally into this position and had slept comfortably and soundly throughout the night.

And he was still sleeping.

Careful not to wake him, she turned beneath his arm, wanting to see him…and smothered a low moan of adoration when she saw his face. Handsome awake, he was absolutely adorable when sleeping, looking more like a tousle-headed toddler than a man in his late thirties. His sandy-brown hair shot from his scalp in wild clumps and flipped endearingly just above his ears. Relaxed in sleep, his lips were slightly parted, the lower one a little puffier than the upper and all but begging for a kiss. A day's worth of stubble shadowed his jaw, chin and upper lip. Lighter than most men's, the blond stubble held the faintest hint of red.

Unable to resist, she touched her lips to his.

He flinched, blinked open his eyes, then smiled and drew her hips to his. "Mornin'."

His voice was rough with sleep, and the huskiness in it sent a shiver sliding down her spine.

"Good morning to you, too. Did you sleep well?"

He nuzzled his cheek to hers. "Like a rock. You?"

Finding the graze of his stubble on her skin unexpectedly erotic, she sighed and snuggled closer. "Never better."

Lulled by the soft stroking of his hand over her buttocks, she closed her eyes, content in the silence that settled over them.

"You never married."

She flipped open her eyes, startled by the unexpected statement. "No, I didn't," she replied, hoping he'd let the topic drop.

"Why?"

Because I never met a man who could make me forget you. That was the answer that came immediately to mind. Probably because it was the truth. But she was hesitant to admit that to him. Why, she wasn't sure, but she suspected it had a lot to do with her pride, which had suffered a mortal blow when he had broken their engagement and married someone else.

She shrugged, hoping by her nonchalance he would assume that she hadn't given the subject much thought. "I guess I just never met anyone I wanted to spend the rest of my life with."

She waited, holding her breath and praying that he wouldn't probe deeper. When he remained silent, his hand still rhythmically stroking her hip, she quietly released the breath and let her eyes close again.

"Do you think you'd want to spend the rest of your life with me?"

Her breath caught in her throat, burned there. Gulping, she slowly lifted her head to look at him. "Was that a rhetorical question or a proposal?"

Gripping her hips more firmly, he shifted her over to lie on top of him. "Since I'm not sure what *rhetorical* means, I'd have to say it was a proposal."

She searched his face, sure that he was teasing her. But

she didn't find even the slightest hint of amusement in his eyes or in his expression. His face was smooth, his eyes a clear crystal blue. If anything, he looked…expectant.

She wasn't ready for this, she thought, feeling the slow burn of panic as it began to crawl through her system. Not yet. Maybe never. She'd agreed to be his friend. They'd become lovers…but husband and wife? *Married?* She gulped as thoughts of all that marrying him would entail flashed through her mind. Giving up her home and business in Dallas. Moving into the house he'd once shared with another woman. Becoming a stepmother.

Dear God, she thought, feeling the revulsion churn in her stomach, making her feel sick. His daughter. The child, whose conception had caused a ripple effect the size of a tidal wave, ripping Wade from her arms and shattering her emotions, her very life. How could she live with that reminder on a daily basis? How could she look that child in the face every day and not be reminded of all that her birth had caused? The anger. The heartbreak. The years lost that she might've shared with Wade. The loneliness. The regret.

"Steph?"

She gulped and made herself focus on his face. Seeing the concern there, she gulped again and eased back to kneel beside him. "I don't know, Wade," she said, trying to keep the tremble from her voice. "This is so unexpected." She pressed a hand to her heart, and gulped again, knowing that *unexpected* didn't even come close to describing her reaction to his proposal. "Everything is still so…new between us. We've only just begun to get to know each other again."

He braced himself up on one elbow and caught her hand. "Nothing's new, Steph. If anything, the feelings I have for you are stronger than they were before. I love you. Always have. And you love me, too. Or at least I think you do."

She dropped her gaze, unable to deny that she did still love him. But *marry* him? Oh, God, she wanted to. More than anything else in the world. But in marrying him, she had to be willing to accept all that he brought to their relationship, including his daughter.

Deciding that she had to be honest with him, she drew in a steadying breath and lifted her head to meet his gaze. "Wade, I do love you," she said and had to stop to swallow back the tears that rose to her throat. "But there's so much more to consider than our feelings for each other."

He wrinkled his brow in confusion. "What could be more important than what we feel for each other?" He squeezed her hand. "I love you, Steph. Everything else is secondary to that."

"Even your daughter?"

He stared, his hand going lax in hers. "Steph, please," he begged. "Don't do this."

She gripped his hand hard, knowing she'd hurt him by mentioning his daughter but desperate to make him understand, to see her side. "It's not that I don't like your daughter, Wade. How could I, when I don't even know her? But she was what tore us apart. Surely you realize how difficult it would be for me to see her, live with her, and not think of that every time I looked at her."

Pulling his hands from hers, he dragged himself to

a sitting position and braced his arms over his knees. "She's just a kid. An innocent kid. You can't blame her for what happened."

"I don't…not intentionally. But she would be a constant reminder." She crawled to lay a hand over his arm, hoping that in touching him she could ease the pain her confession was causing him. "I don't want to hurt you, Wade. I would never do anything to purposely hurt you. But I can't lie to you either. Your daughter presents a problem for me, and I can't promise you that I can accept her or even feel comfortable living in the same house with her."

"But you don't even know her," he said in frustration. "If you met her, spent some time with her, you might find you like her a lot."

"That's just it. I don't want to meet her. Not yet," she added quickly. She took his hands and grasped them between her own. "We've only just begun to heal old wounds and make a new start. Maybe in time…"

He searched her face. "So that's not a definite no? I mean, about marrying me."

"It's a maybe. A really strong I-want-this-to-work-out-too kind of maybe."

He opened his knees and dragged her up his chest. "I can live with one of those kind of maybes." Smiling, he swept her hair back from her face. "You're gonna like her," he said confidently. "Once you two meet, I just know that you're going to get along great."

Six

Scowling, Wade shoved the plate of pancakes in front of Meghan. "I said no, and begging isn't going to make me change my mind."

"But, Daddy!" she cried and jumped up from the table to follow him to the sink. "It's going to be the coolest party ever. Richie's parents have hired a DJ and everything!"

He shoved his hands into the dishwater. "Richie is fifteen years old," he reminded her.

"So? I'm going to be thirteen my next birthday."

"Which is still six months away." Frustrated, he dropped the pan he was scrubbing and turned to face her. "You're too young to be running around with guys Richie's age and you're definitely too young to date. Now the answer is no, and don't ask me again."

She pushed her hands into fists at her sides. "I hate

you and I wish you weren't my daddy!" Whirling, she ran from the room, sobbing uncontrollably.

Wade braced his hands against the edge of the sink and drew in a long breath. She didn't mean it, he told himself as he slowly released the breath. She was just mad. Blowing off steam. Kids said things like that all the time to their parents when they didn't get their way.

Setting his jaw, he picked up the pan again and began to scrub. She'd get over it. It wasn't as if it was the end of the world. There'd be other parties for her to go to. Other boys for her to date.

He glanced over his shoulder to the hallway beyond the kitchen and the empty staircase that stretched to the second floor.

But damn if being a parent wasn't hell.

Stephanie tossed the tattered book on veterinary medicine into the box marked Trash.

"Hey!" Frowning, Wade shifted to dig it out. "You can't throw that away."

"Why not? I have no use for it, and the library won't accept books in that bad a condition."

He smoothed a hand over the worn cover. "But this was like Bud's bible. Passed down to him from his father. He referred to it whenever any of his livestock fell sick."

She waved an impatient hand. "Then you take it. You have more use for it than I ever will." Rising to her knees, she pulled another stack of books from the shelves, then sat down to sort them.

His forehead creased in a frown, Wade watched her, wondering how she could be so indifferent about something that had belonged to her father, a book that Bud had cherished as much as another man might have gold. Giving his head a shake, he turned away and placed the book near the door so that he wouldn't forget to take it with him when he left.

"Bud had the weirdest reading taste," he heard Steph say and glanced her way.

Propped up on her knees, her elbows on the floor and her chin on her fists, she read the titles imprinted on the spines of the books stacked in front of her. "*Moby Dick, How to Win Friends and Influence People, Mommie Dearest.* And a couple of dime-store Westerns." She shook her head. "Weird."

"Well-rounded," he argued.

"Weird," she repeated, then picked up the books and dumped them in the Donate box. Dusting off her hands, she turned for the closet. "I guess I've put off dealing with his clothes long enough."

She opened the door and scooped up an armload of clothing and lifted, making sure the hooks had cleared the rod before turning and heaving the stack onto the bed. She picked up a coat, gave it a cursory once-over, then tossed it in the trash.

Wade dug it right back out.

She huffed a breath. "Wade, I threw that away."

"And I took it out," he informed her.

"Why? It's covered with stains and the cuffs are all frayed."

"It was Bud's favorite."

"That doesn't make it any less a rag!"

He folded the coat neatly in half and laid it in the Donate box.

"Wade!" Stephanie cried. "What are you doing? Nobody's gonna want Bud's old coat."

"There's nothing wrong with that coat. Just because it's seen some miles doesn't mean it can't keep a body warm. Besides, I think Bud would be pleased to know that somebody got some use out of it."

"Whatever," she mumbled, then picked up a shirt and laughed. "Oh, my gosh. Do you remember this?" she asked and held it up for Wade to see. The shirt's front sported a bold red-and-white-stripe fabric, the back a blue with white stars embroidered in neat rows. "Bud wore it to every Fourth of July parade ever since I can remember."

Wade dropped the sack of trash he'd just picked up and fisted his hands on his hips. "And I suppose you're going to throw that away, too?"

She looked at him in puzzlement. "Why would I keep it?"

"Because it was *his?* Because it was something that Bud obviously liked?"

Seeing her stunned expression, he turned away, dragged a hand over his hair, then spun back, unable to suppress the frustration he'd carried since his battle with Meghan that morning. "Do you realize that you never say *my father* or *my dad* when you refer to Bud? You say *Bud.*"

She opened her hands. "So? That was his name."

"But you never used it before! You always called him Dad, never Bud."

"What difference does it make what I call him? You know who I'm talking about."

"It doesn't make any difference to me, but it would probably make a helluva lot to Bud! Can you imagine how hurt he would be if he could hear you right now? Calling him *Bud* and throwing away the things he cherished most. For God's sake, Steph! He was your father, not an acquaintance."

Seeing her hurt expression and knowing he'd gone too far, he stopped and hauled in a breath through his nose. "I'm sorry," he said, releasing it. "I didn't mean any of that."

"Obviously you did or you wouldn't have said it in the first place."

Frustrated, he dragged a hand over his hair again, then dropped it to his side. "It's just that you seem to have forgotten that Bud was your dad. He was the one who raised you, took care of you. But ever since you found those letters, all you can talk about is your *real* dad."

"I haven't forgotten Bud," she said defensively. "I loved him. I will *always* love him. But I owe a certain allegiance to my real father, too. And the only reason I refer to Dad as Bud is for clarification. I have *two* fathers," she reminded him. "My natural one and the one who adopted me. Just because I'm determined to get to know my natural father in no way detracts from my feelings for the one who raised me."

Realizing how much he'd upset her, Wade gathered her into his arms. "I'm sorry," he murmured with real regret. "I guess I'm just a little touchy about fathers in general because of what Meghan said to me this morning."

She drew back to frown up at him. "What did she say?"

He ducked his head, reluctant to repeat his daughter's angry words. "That she hated me."

"What?" Steph cried.

"She didn't mean it," he hurried to assure her. "She

was just mad because I wouldn't let her go to a party with a guy three years older than her."

"But, Wade—"

He silenced her with a kiss. "Forget it," he said and turned away. "They're just words. And you know the old saying about sticks and stones...."

Stephanie hummed along with the song playing on the radio as she sorted through the linens she'd pulled from the closet. Most she tossed into the Donate box, as there was very little sentiment to be attached to sheets and towels. But the tablecloths, especially those crocheted by her grandmother, she placed in a separate pile, planning to keep.

"A lost art," she murmured and paused to finger the decorative filet crochet border on a set of linen napkins, trying to remember who had made them. All of the women on her mother's side of the family had done some type of handiwork. Whether it was quilting, knitting, crocheting or embroidery, each had excelled at her chosen craft and had generously shared the fruits of her labors with other family members.

"Aunt Colleen," she decided and set the napkins in the Keeper stack.

A knock on the door had her lifting her head to peer toward the front of the house. Glancing at her wristwatch, she frowned as she hurried down the hall, wondering who it could be. It was too early for Wade's daily visit, plus he'd told her he'd probably be late because he was working his cattle this morning. Murmuring a fervent prayer that it wasn't Mrs. Snodgrass, the nosiest busybody at her mother's church, she opened the door.

She lifted a brow in surprise when she found Wade standing on the porch. She sputtered a laugh. "And since when have you ever knocked?" She opened the door wider. "You're lucky I even answered the door. I almost didn't because I was afraid it might be Mrs. Snodgrass."

When he made no move to enter, she looked at him curiously and noticed the tension in his face. "Is something wrong?" she asked in concern.

"You could say that," he replied tersely, then released a long breath. "I need a favor." He gestured behind him to where his truck was parked. "Meghan's in the truck, and I'd appreciate it if you would keep an eye on her for me."

"Meghan?" she repeated, her stomach knotting in dread. "But—shouldn't she be in school?"

He set his jaw. "*Should* being the operative word. She got expelled this morning." He gave her a pleading look. "I know it's asking a lot, considering, but it would only be for a couple of hours."

"Why can't she stay at home? Surely she's old enough to leave by herself."

"I don't trust her, okay?" he said, his frustration returning. "She's already threatened to run away. If I leave her at home, the minute I'm out of sight, I'm afraid she'll haul butt."

Stephanie glanced toward the truck and tried not to wring her hands. "I don't know, Wade," she said uneasily. "What if she pulls a stunt while she's here? I wouldn't know what to do."

"You can call me. I've got my cell." Before she could think of another excuse or alternative to offer, he turned for his truck.

"Wade!" she cried, reaching out a hand as if to stop him.

But it was too late. He already had the passenger door open and a young girl was climbing down. Petite and with long blond hair styled with the sides pulled up and gathered into a clip at the crown of her head, she didn't look like the kind of person who would get expelled from school. She looked more like one of the little girls that came to Stephanie's door selling Girl Scout cookies…or at least she did until Wade took her arm and started her toward the house, and Stephanie got a look at the belligerent expression on her face.

Stephanie gulped once, then gulped again. She'd thought she didn't want to meet Wade's daughter before. Now she was sure of it.

Stephanie led the way into the den. "Would you like something to drink?"

Meghan dropped down on the sofa in a slouch. "I'm not thirsty."

Racking her brain to think what to do with the child, Stephanie saw the remote for the TV and reached for it. "How about watching some television?"

"Whatever."

Irritated by the girl's surly attitude, Stephanie slapped the remote on the coffee table in front of her. "Well, here's the remote, if you decide to. I'll be in the back, packing. If you need anything, you can find me there."

Halfway down the hall, she heard the TV click on, followed by spurts of different sounds as Meghan surfed through the channels. "Delinquent," she muttered under her breath. No wonder the child had been expelled from school. With an attitude like hers, it was amazing she was allowed to attend at all.

As she passed her bedroom door, she heard the musical peal of her cell phone and ducked inside to retrieve it from the bedside table. Checking the display, she smiled when she recognized Kiki's number.

"Hey, Kiki," she said, bringing the phone to her ear. "How's motherhood?"

"Don't ask. When are you coming home? I don't know how much longer I can take all this togetherness before I start tearing out my hair."

Laughing, Stephanie sank down on the edge of her bed. "What have the twins done now?"

"What *haven't* they done," Kiki shot back, then heaved a weary sigh. "I don't want to talk about the twins. It's too depressing. Tell me what you're doing."

Stephanie cast an uneasy glance toward the door, then stood and tiptoed to her bathroom. "Babysitting a juvenile delinquent," she whispered as she closed the door behind her.

"What? Speak up. I can't hear you."

"Babysitting a juvenile delinquent," she whispered a little louder.

"Who?"

"Wade's daughter."

"What!"

Being as Kiki was one of only a handful of people in Dallas who knew about Stephanie's past relationship with Wade, Stephanie could understand her friend's shock. "I know. Crazy, isn't it?"

"Does this mean you and Wade are…?"

She sagged down onto the commode seat. "I don't know what we are," she said miserably. "We've established a truce of sorts, but—" She glanced at the door, then turned her head toward the tub, fearing Meghan might be able to hear her, and said in a low voice, "His daughter's a problem."

"Because she's a juvenile delinquent?"

She frowned, a visual of Meghan's belligerent expression popping into her mind. "That, too," she muttered, then sighed. "But can you imagine what it would be like to have to look at her every day and know, if not for her, Wade and I would be married right now?"

"Did you tell Wade that?"

"Yes."

"Please, God," Kiki begged, "tell me you didn't."

Stephanie frowned at the dread in Kiki's voice. "Of course I did. There was no point in lying."

"Oh, no," Kiki moaned, then cried, "Steph, what were you thinking? That's his daughter, for cripes' sake! You can't tell a parent something like that. It's the same as telling him his child is ugly!"

"It is not," Stephanie replied defensively. "Besides, Wade knows she's not perfect. Heck, she was expelled from school! That's why he brought her over here in the first place."

"It doesn't matter," Kiki argued. "A parent can think or say anything they want to about his kid, but let someone else make a derogatory comment, and that same parent will fight to the death to defend the kid."

Stephanie caught her lip between her teeth. She knew that she'd hurt Wade's feelings with her refusal to meet his daughter, but what other choice had she had? He'd asked her to marry him. There was no way she could have refused his proposal without telling him why.

"He understood," she said, trying to convince herself it was true.

"Uh-huh," Kiki said doubtfully. "I'll just bet he did."

"He did," she insisted, then pushed to her feet and crossed to the window to look out. "I told him that maybe in time I would feel differently. There's still so much that he and I have to work through. Everything is so new, so—" Her eyes flipped wide and she whipped the drape back for a better view. "Oh, my God!" she cried, then whirled for the door. "Kiki, I've got to go."

"Why? What's wrong?"

"Meghan's running away!"

Before Kiki could ask any more questions, Stephanie tossed the phone onto the bed and ran out of her room, down the hall.

Once outside, she broke into a full run. "Meghan!" she shouted, racing after the girl. "Where do you think you're going?"

Meghan glanced back over her shoulder, her eyes wide in alarm, then took off at a run. Stephanie raced after her. "Meghan, stop!" she yelled.

Meghan stumbled, fell, then scrambled to her feet and ran again. Her fall, coupled with the awkward backpack she was carrying, gave Stephanie the edge she needed to close the distance between them.

With her lungs burning, her arms pumping like pistons, she knew she had only one chance to stop the girl. She dived, tackling Meghan around the legs and bringing her down.

Meghan twisted beneath her, trying to fight free. "Let me go!"

Gasping, Stephanie rocked back on her heels but

kept a firm grip on Meghan's arm. "Uh-uh. You're staying right here with me."

"You can't tell me what to do," Meghan yelled angrily. "You're not my mother."

"Thank heaven for that," Stephanie muttered under her breath, then gave Meghan's arm a yank and all but dragged her back to the house.

By the time they reached the porch, Meghan was sobbing. Setting her jaw against the heartbreaking sound, Stephanie marched her into the house and to the den. She released Meghan's arm and pointed a stiff finger at the sofa. "Sit."

Sniffling, Meghan flopped down on the sofa.

Stephanie yanked tissues from the box on the coffee table and pushed them into the girl's hand. "I don't know where you thought you were going, but I'm telling you right now that you better not pull that stunt again. Understand?"

Her chin on her chest, Meghan sniffed, nodded, then lifted her head. "Are you going to tell my dad?" she asked hesitantly.

It was Stephanie's first real good look at the child. Though dirt and tears smeared her face, she could see that she was pretty. White-blond hair hung past her shoulders and framed an oval face. Her eyes, the color of roasted chestnuts, were large, and her tear-spiked lashes were thick and long. In spite of her desire not to, Stephanie found herself searching for a resemblance to Wade but found nothing in the child's features that even remotely reminded her of Wade.

"Are you?" Meghan prodded.

Stephanie firmed her lips, refusing to be suckered by

the girl's puppy-dog look. "Your father entrusted you to my care. Your running away makes me look irresponsible, incompetent, and I don't think that's fair, do you?"

Meghan hung her head. "No, ma'am," she murmured.

Stephanie didn't know if the child's contriteness was an act to draw pity or if she really did feel badly for what she'd done. Whatever her reasons, Stephanie wasn't about to take a chance on her running away again.

"As punishment for disobeying your father's instructions, you're going to help me."

"What do I have to do?"

"Pack." Stephanie motioned for Meghan to follow her. "I've been going through the linen closet," she said tersely as she led the way down the hall. "I've already—" Realizing that Meghan wasn't following, she turned to look behind her and saw that Meghan had stopped in front of her parents' bedroom. "Meghan?" she said in frustration. "What are you doing?"

The girl turned to look at her, and Stephanie was shocked to see that her eyes were filled with tears again.

"What's wrong?" she asked in concern.

Meghan dragged a hand beneath her eyes. "It's just that I haven't been here since Mr. Calloway died and I guess I forgot for a minute, 'cause I expected to see him lying in his bed."

Stephanie gulped, knowing that this was no act. No one could fake the depth of sadness she saw reflected in the child's eyes. "Yeah, I know," she said as she walked to stand with her. "Sometimes I catch myself listening for him, especially around dinnertime."

Sliding an arm around the girl, she urged her away from the door and down the hall. "Did you visit him very often?" she asked, hoping to distract the girl from the image that must surely be stuck in her mind of Bud lying sick in bed.

Meghan lifted a shoulder. "Not too much after he got sick." She pursed her lips. "Daddy was afraid I'd wear him out with my talking."

Chuckling, Stephanie removed a stack of linens from the floor, then sat down on the floor, her back to the wall, and patted the space next to her. "Have a seat," she invited.

Meghan sank down with a youthful ease that Stephanie couldn't help envying.

"So you're a talker, huh?" Stephanie said as she began to sort through the stack of pillowcases.

Meghan stretched her legs out in front of her and tapped the tip of her tennis shoes together. "Daddy seems to think so."

"I guess you knew my mother, too," Stephanie said, curious to discover how well Wade's daughter knew her parents.

"Yeah. When I was little, sometimes she would keep me when I was too sick to go to school and Daddy had something he needed to do." She plucked absently at a thread on her jeans. "When I had chicken pox, I was itching real bad, and she made me an oatmeal bath to soak in. She was always doing nice things like that."

Stephanie had to swallow back emotion before she could reply, ashamed of the resentment she'd felt toward her mother. "Yes, she had a kind heart." Forcing a smile, she picked up one of the stacks of pillowcases she had sorted and passed it to Meghan. "These go in that box over there," she said, pointing. "The one marked Donate."

Hopping up, Meghan moved to place the linens in the box, then returned to sit at Stephanie's side again.

Feeling the child's stare, Stephanie glanced over at her. "What?"

"I was just wondering how come I've never seen you before."

Stephanie quickly looked away. "Well," she said, stalling while she tried to think of a plausible explanation to offer. "I live in Dallas and own a business there. It keeps me pretty busy."

"What kind of business?"

"I'm a photo stylist."

Meghan wrinkled her brow. "What's that?"

Stephanie set the linens she held on her lap, wondering how best to describe her job to a young girl. "You know the advertisements you see in magazines? The ones that have photographs?"

"Yeah."

"I set the scenes for the pictures. I gather all the props, set everything up, then the photographer—and the models, if any are needed—come in and the photographer takes the pictures."

Meghan stared, her eyes wide in wonder. "How cool is that!"

Stephanie chuckled. "It is a cool job. But it can also be a royal pain in the patootee."

"Patootee?" Meghan repeated, then fell over on the floor, laughing. "That's the lamest word I've ever heard."

Stephanie lifted a brow. "Beats getting my mouth washed out with soap for using the more popular expression."

Her eyes rounding, Meghan pushed up to her elbows.

"You mean, Mrs. Calloway washed your mouth out with soap?"

"She certainly did," Stephanie said with a decisive nod. "But it only took twice before I learned not to say words that she didn't approve of."

"Wow."

Amused by the girl's shocked look, Stephanie shook her head and reached for another stack of linens. "So what's your punishment for saying bad words?"

Meghan blinked, then shrugged. "There's not one."

Stephanie gave her a sideways glance. "Oh, please. Surely your father doesn't allow you to say curse words."

"He doesn't exactly *allow* me to curse, but if I slip and say something I shouldn't in front of him, he just gives me a mean look and says, 'You better watch your mouth, young lady.'"

Her impersonation of Wade was so funny Stephanie couldn't help but laugh. "Maybe I should give him some pointers I picked up from my mother."

Meghan grimaced. "Yeah, like he could be any meaner. He rags on me all the time about the way I dress and the music I listen to. And I don't *dare* have the channel turned to MTV when he's at home. If I do, he goes ballistic."

Stephanie drew back to peer at her, unsure whether she should believe her or not. "That doesn't sound like the Wade I know."

"You know my daddy?"

Realizing her mistake, Stephanie looked away and busied herself straightening linens. "He moved to the ranch next door while I was in college," she replied vaguely.

"Do you know my mom, too?"

It was all Stephanie could do to remain upright. "No, I've never met your mother. I was living in Dallas when your parents married."

"Oh," Meghan said, sounding disappointed.

Anxious to change the subject, Stephanie asked, "Are you thirsty?" She heaved herself up from the floor. "I know I am. Let's get a soda."

"Okay."

Stephanie led the way to the kitchen, with Meghan following close on her heels. Just as she stepped inside, the back door opened and Wade walked in.

"Well, hi," she said in surprise. "Meghan and I were about to have a soda. Would you like one?"

"Maybe next time." He tipped his head, indicating his daughter. "Did she give you any trouble?"

Stephanie glanced down and met Meghan's gaze. Seeing the girl's fear, she gave her a reassuring smile. "Nothing I couldn't handle."

Wade shifted his gaze between the two, his expression doubtful, then heaved a sigh and motioned for Meghan to join him. "Come on," he said, already turning for the door. "We need to go."

"Couldn't I stay here with Stephanie?" Meghan asked. "I was helping her pack."

"No, we've got—" He hesitated a moment, then said, "Company waiting."

Meghan's eyes lit with hope. "Mom's here?"

Wade pushed through the door and stepped outside without answering.

Meghan let out an excited squeal and ran after him. At the door she stopped and glanced back. "Thanks for not ratting me out."

Stephanie leveled a finger at her in warning. "Just don't make me regret it."

Meghan grinned. "I won't," she said, then charged out the door, shouting, "Hey, Dad! Wait for me!"

Stephanie tried not to think about Wade's ex being at his house.

But it was hopeless. Every time she pushed the thought from her mind, it dug a new hole and came crawling back in. Deciding that a nice hot bath was what she needed to get Wade's ex off her mind, she headed for her bathroom and turned on the tap. She was stripping off her clothes when her cell phone rang. Grabbing a towel to drape around her, she hurried into the bedroom to answer it.

"Hello," she said breathlessly.

"Were you just going to leave me hanging?"

She winced at the annoyance in Kiki's voice. "Sorry. I've been sort of busy."

"So did the runaway make good her escape?"

Remembering she'd left the water running in the bathroom, Stephanie retraced her steps. "No. I caught her. But I had to tackle her from behind and drag her to the ground to stop her."

"You've got to be kidding!" Kiki cried, then hooted a laugh. "Oh, to have been a fly on the wall and seen that."

Rather proud of her accomplishment, Stephanie buffed her nails against her chest. "It was a clever save, even if I do say so myself."

"Congratulations. Now tell me the good stuff. Why did Wade bring her to you, of all people? Does she know about you and Wade? Did she say anything about her mother? I want the dirt, so start shoveling."

Shaking her head at her friend's outrageousness, Stephanie squirted bath oil beneath the tap. "Has anyone ever told you that you're nosy?"

"Daily. Now spill."

Stephanie tested the water, then dropped the towel and climbed in. "I don't know why Wade brought her here, but I'd guess it was because he had nowhere else to take her. He was in the middle of vaccinating his cattle and couldn't keep an eye on her himself."

"Why didn't he just leave her at home? Good grief. Surely the kid's old enough to stay by herself."

"She is," Stephanie agreed. "But he doesn't trust her. He said she'd threatened to run away."

"Wow. I thought you were exaggerating when you said you were babysitting a juvenile delinquent. Obviously you were being serious."

Growing thoughtful, Stephanie lifted a toe to pop a bubble. "I may be wrong—God knows I don't have any experience with children—but I don't think she's really a bad kid. She certainly doesn't look the part. She has really long white-blond hair and the biggest eyes. She looks…well, almost angelic."

Remembering the belligerent expression on her face when Wade had first dropped her off, she added, "But she has the potential to turn bad. I got a peek of a darker side when Wade first dropped her off. Angry. Hostile. Rebellious. If he doesn't get her in hand fairly soon, I would think she could easily turn into a huge problem for him."

"Bet you five he's suffering from the Guilty Parent Syndrome."

Stephanie choked out a laugh. "The *what?*"

"Guilty Parent Syndrome. You see it all the time in divorce cases. Wade's the one who asked for the divorce, right?"

"That was the talk around town."

"Right. So he's taking heat from the daughter because she blames him for making her mother leave. He feels sorry for the kid, so he goes easy on her, trying to make it up to her. If the kid's smart—and it sounds like she is—she picks up on his guilt and plays him like a piano, and the cycle continues until—bingo!—the kid is a holy terror and totally out of control."

Shaking her head, Stephanie slid farther down into the bubbles. "You need to quit working for me and hang out a shingle. You'd make an excellent psychologist."

"Comes from all the years I spent in therapy."

Stephanie frowned. "Your mother should have been the one in therapy, not you."

"Try telling her that."

Stephanie shuddered at the thought of having any conversation with Kiki's neurotic mother. "Thanks, but I think I'll pass."

"What about the kid's mother? Wade's ex? Did the kid say anything about her?"

"Nothing specific, though she did ask if I knew her."

Kiki whistled softly. "Man, this just gets crazier and crazier. Like a soap opera."

"Tell me about it," Stephanie muttered drily. "The ex is at his house right now."

"Why? Is it her weekend to have the kid or something?"

"How would I know?" Stephanie snapped. "I just know she's there."

"Do I detect a hint of jealousy?"

"Why would I be jealous? They're divorced."

"Which doesn't mean squat. He might be through with her, but that doesn't mean she's through with him."

Since that was the exact thought that Stephanie had hoped to escape by taking a bubble bath, she remained silent, refusing to discuss it.

"Steph?"

"Yes?" she said tersely.

"Just wanted to make sure you were still there."

"I am."

"And obviously don't want to talk about his ex," Kiki deducted, then sighed her disappointment. "Okay, so tell me what you think about the kid after spending the morning with her."

"She's your average twelve-year-old," Stephanie replied, then amended, "except for the ugly rebellious streak."

"So you liked her?"

Stephanie considered the question for a moment and was surprised to find that she did like Meghan. "She's okay," she replied vaguely. "And obviously crazy about her mother."

"Which would make you the ugly stepmother if you and Wade should work things out."

Stephanie scowled, not having to stretch very far to imagine the kind of problems that could create for her and Wade. "Thanks, Kiki. I really appreciate you bringing that to my attention."

"Sorry," Kiki mumbled, then brightened. "But look

at it this way. The kid won't be around forever. She's twelve, so she should be leaving the nest in another five or six years. Then you and Wade would be alone."

If their relationship lasted that long, Stephanie thought sadly. Sharing a house with another woman's child and a bed with that child's father had the potential to destroy even the strongest of relationships.

Giving herself a shake, she said to Kiki, "There's no sense in worrying about that. Wade and I aren't married. We're just…friends."

"Steph?"

Stephanie jumped at the sound of Wade's voice, almost dropping the phone in the water. "In here," she called, then brought the phone back to her ear and whispered frantically to Kiki, "I've got to go. Wade's here."

"Friends, huh?" Kiki snorted a laugh. "I'd say you're more than friends, since you just invited him into the bathroom while you're in the tub."

"Goodbye, Kiki," Stephanie said firmly, then disconnected the phone.

Just as Stephanie leaned to lay the phone on the commode seat, Wade stepped into the bathroom. He stood there a moment, staring, then started toward the tub, unbuttoning his shirt.

Stephanie sputtered a nervous laugh. "What are you doing?"

His gaze on hers, he flipped back his belt buckle and pulled down the zipper on his jeans. "What does it look like I'm doing?"

She watched as he hooked the toe of one boot behind the heel of the other and pried it off, then lifted her gaze to his. "Stripping?" she asked meekly.

He pushed his jeans down his hips, kicked them aside. "No." He gave her a nudge and slipped into the tub behind her. "I'm bathing."

"But where's Meghan?"

He slid his arms around her waist and pressed his lips to the curve of her neck. "At home."

Since he'd claimed he didn't trust Meghan to stay alone, she had to assume her mother was there with her. Although she didn't find that thought at all comforting, Wade was with her, which had to say something about his preferences. She angled her head, giving him better access to her neck. "How long can you stay?"

He dragged his lips down to her shoulder. Nipped. "As long as it takes."

She closed her eyes, stifling a groan. "As long as what takes?" she asked breathlessly.

He turned her around to face him and sent water splashing over the edge. His blue eyes, dark with passion, burned through hers as he drew her legs around his waist. "To satisfy this hunger I have for you."

Water lapped against her body, adding to the sensations created by his erection nudging her belly. Looping her arms around his neck, she smiled as she lowered her face to his. "That might take a while."

"Yeah." He released a sigh against her lips. "That's what I'm hoping."

Later, snuggled against Wade in her bed, Stephanie found herself thinking about something Meghan had said to her that morning. "Wade?" she said hesitantly.

More asleep than awake, he hummed a lazy response.

"Meghan said something this morning that concerns me."

He groaned and buried his face between her breasts. "Please tell me she wasn't rude."

Biting back a smile at the dread she heard in his voice, she ran her fingers through his hair to reassure him. "No, though I have to admit, when you first dropped her off, she was sporting a pretty tough attitude."

Sighing, he drew his head back and placed it on the pillow opposite hers. "She's *always* sporting an attitude. That's nothing new."

"This has nothing to do with her attitude. It's something she said."

"What?"

"We were talking about cursing, and I told her that when I said a curse word, my mother would wash my mouth out with soap."

He smiled softly, as if at a fond memory. "My mom did that, too."

"Meghan said that when she says a bad word, you don't punish her."

"I damn sure do," he said defensively, then waved away Stephanie's concern. "She was pulling your leg, blowing hot air."

"I don't think so." Stephanie knew she was taking a chance on alienating Wade by discussing his daughter with him, but Meghan's comment concerned her enough that she felt she should speak her mind. "She said you only give her a mean look and tell her to watch her mouth."

His brows drew together. "So? That's the same as telling her I don't approve of that kind of talk."

Stephanie laid a hand against his chest, hoping to take the sting out of what she was about to say. "Maybe you need to be a little more firm. Let her know that in the future there will be specific consequences for bad behavior."

"And you think washing her mouth out with soap is going to keep her from cussing?" He snorted a breath. "Sure as hell didn't break me."

She pursed her lips. "Obviously not. The point is, Meghan doesn't seem to think there are any consequences for her actions. A mean look from you isn't enough of a deterrent. You need to be firmer with her. Establish rules and set specific punishments to be implemented when she breaks them."

He lifted a brow. "Oh? And how many children have you raised?"

For a moment Stephanie could only stare, his careless remark cutting deeply. "I haven't," she said and rolled away, swinging her legs over the side of the bed. "I was only offering an opinion after spending some time with your daughter."

He caught her arm, stopping her before she could stand. "Hey," he said softly. "I didn't mean that the way it sounded."

When she kept her face averted, refusing to look at him, he tugged her down to lie beside him again. "I'm sorry, Steph." He laid a hand on her cheek. "You're probably right. Maybe I am too easy on Meghan. But sometimes I just flat don't know what to do with her. You have no idea what kind of crap kids are getting into these days. Body piercings and tattoos, not to mention sex and drugs. She's twelve going on twenty-two. I try to keep a tight rein on her, hoping to keep her out of trouble. But she kicks and screams about how strict I am and threatens to run away and live with her mother. I'm afraid if I come down on her too hard, she will."

"Maybe she should live with her mother."

By the look on Wade's face, Stephanie knew she'd said the wrong thing.

"Wade," she said and reached for him, wanting to explain.

He shoved her hand aside and rolled from the bed and to his feet to face her. "You think her mother would do a better job of raising her?" he asked angrily. Without waiting for an answer, he strode to the bathroom, scooped up his clothes and returned, jerking on his jeans. "Well, let me tell you something Dr. Know-It-All," he said, pointing a stiff finger at her face. "On my worst day I'm a better parent than Angela will ever be. I fought for custody of Meghan for that very reason and won. Angela's nothing but a—" He clamped his lips together and spun for the door, pulling on his shirt.

Stephanie bolted from the bed and grabbed a robe, shrugging it on as she ran after him.

"Wade, wait!"

He didn't even slow down.

She caught up with him at the front door and grabbed his arm. When he tried to jerk free, she tightened her grip. "No," she said, her anger rising to match his. "You're not leaving until I have a chance to explain. I wasn't suggesting that you are a bad parent. Meghan's a *girl,* Wade, and a young girl needs her mother. If she were a boy, maybe it would be different. But she's not a boy. She's a *girl* and she's at an age where she needs to talk about things that she may not feel comfortable talking about with you. That's why I said what I did. I was simply suggesting that maybe she needs a mother right now more than she does a father. I wasn't suggesting that her mother is a better parent than you. How could I? I don't even know the woman."

He grabbed her arms, making her blink in surprise. "No, you don't know her. If you did, you'd understand why I've fought so hard to keep Meghan away from her. Why I insist that a court-appointed guardian be present at all times when she visits Meghan. Angela is a drug addict, a whore who'll sell herself to any man who'll give her another fix."

He dropped his hands from her arms and took a step back, suddenly looking tired, beaten. "Do you know how I know that, Steph?" he asked quietly. "I know because I was once one of those men."

Seven

Stephanie walked around in a daze the next morning, still numbed by Wade's confession. She couldn't believe he'd ever been the kind of man he'd described. Sure, when they'd first started dating, he'd told her a little about his life prior to his move to the ranch next to her parents. How he'd gone a little crazy after his parents' deaths and done some things he wasn't proud of. But Wade involved in drugs? Associating with a woman like the one he described Angela to be? She couldn't believe it. He was so straight, so *good*.

Frustrated by her inability to come to grips with the man he'd described to her, she moved to the front window and looked out. What difference does it make if he had done those things? she asked herself. He wasn't the same person he was back then. That was all in the past. He'd changed, made a fresh start. He was a good person, kind. Hadn't he looked out for Bud after her mother had died? Hadn't he comforted Stephanie when he'd found her crying over her father's letters? Hadn't he fought for custody of his daughter, wanting to protect her from the environment in which her mother lived? A man who did those things wasn't a bad person. He was good and kind.

She should've told him that, she realized with a suddenness that clutched at her chest. She shouldn't have let him walk out of her house without telling him that his past didn't matter. That he was a wonderful man, kind and generous, and that she loved him with all her heart.

She glanced at her watch and was surprised to see that it was past noon, the time that Wade usually dropped off a bundle of letters for her to read. Praying that nothing had happened at home that would have prevented him from leaving, she hurried to the front door, wanting to make sure he hadn't gone on to the barn and pastures without stopping first.

Two steps onto the porch her left foot connected with something hard, making her stumble. Catching herself from falling, she glanced down to see what she'd tripped over and found a box sitting on the porch. Her heart seemed to stop for a moment when she recognized it as the one Wade had used the night he'd carried away the bundles of her father's letters.

She stooped to pick it up, wondering why he'd left it for her to find rather than bringing it inside. And why would he drop off the entire box instead of the usual single bundle?

She gulped, afraid she already knew the answer. She'd let him leave the night before without telling him that his past didn't matter to her, without assuring him of her love. She'd even suggested he allow his daughter to live with his ex, told him that she couldn't consider marrying him because she couldn't bear the thought of living with the child who would serve as a daily reminder of the choice Wade had made and all the hurt she'd suffered at his hand.

She'd let him down. When he'd needed her most, she had denied him her love, her understanding, and instead chose to batter him with the resentment she had hoarded through the years, the bitterness she had clung to.

Her heart heavy, her eyes filled with tears of regret, she gathered the box close and went back inside.

Janine,
I don't know how I survived the year I spent in Vietnam before I met you. Your letters are what keep me going, what help me deal with the tragedy and death I see every day.

I've just about worn out the pictures of you I brought with me. I can't tell you the number of times a day I pull them out just to look at them, to remind myself that there is a world beyond the hell I'm living in right now, one where there is normalcy, laughter and love.

Sometimes it's hard to remember what it's like back home. To sleep without being afraid someone is going to slip up on you in the night and slit your throat. To walk without fear of stepping on a mine or a booby trap. To be able to eat food other than C-rations. To wear clothes that aren't all but rotting off my body.

I don't understand this war. Why people would want to kill each other. Surely there's a better way to resolve differences, to make peace between nations and keep it. The loss of lives—on both sides—is unimaginable, and that's without considering the lives of the people that are destroyed or changed forever by the loss of their loved ones.

A couple of guys I knew back home went to Canada to avoid the draft. At the time I remember thinking they were cowards for choosing to leave their country rather than fight for it. Now I'm not so sure. I still don't believe I ever would've run, even knowing what I know now. But I don't feel the same about the guys who did choose to run. I don't consider them cowards anymore. Doing what they did took courage. Granted, it was a different kind of courage than the one required to stand and fight. But it took guts to do what they did. Leaving your home and family behind and knowing that you may never see them again... well, that takes a certain kind of courage, too. In some ways, it's the same sacrifice or chance a soldier makes when he puts on a uniform and goes to war.

Unable to read any more, Stephanie let the letter drop to her lap and stared out the window at the darkness beyond the house. Her father had only been twenty-one when he'd written the letter, yet there was a wisdom in his words, a wealth of experience which exceeded that of most men his age. Women, too, she thought. At twenty-one she'd been in her third year of college and living in an apartment in Dallas, near the campus of Southern Methodist University, and without a care in the world. Her education was paid for by her parents, who covered her living expenses, as well, which allowed her to focus on her studies without worrying about supporting herself. The only fear she had faced was making good grades in the courses she was enrolled in, and the only tragedy she'd suffered was when Wade had broken their engagement.

The latter had been devastating and it had taken weeks, months even, for her to drag herself from the depression that losing him had plunged her into. But she hadn't resurfaced fully healed or unscathed from the occurrence. From the darkness she'd brought with her her resentment toward Wade, and used it like a talisman to keep herself from ever being hurt again.

The broken engagement had changed her life in so many ways…most not very flattering. She'd remained in Dallas but had withdrawn from her classes, which had put her a semester behind in graduating. For months she'd refused to come home, unable to bear the thought of possibly bumping into Wade and his new wife. She'd let that fear control her actions for years, making only brief visits home to see her parents and, while there, refusing to step so much as a foot outside their house.

And she'd allowed the breakup to affect more than just her family life. For more than a year she had refused to go out on any of the dates her friends set up for her. And when she had finally begun dating again, she'd kept a firm grip on her emotions, her feelings, determined to never let a man hurt her again.

But the most regrettable fallout from their breakup

was holding on to her anger with Wade and never forgiving him for hurting her. In the days immediately following their breakup she'd refused to see him or talk to him. It was easy enough to do. She'd simply monitored her phone calls and deleted the messages he'd left on her answering machine without listening to them, tore up the letters he'd sent without ever opening them.

She dropped her chin in shame as she realized the domino effect her stubbornness and bitterness had had on the people she loved most—as well as many whose lives she'd touched only briefly. By stubbornly refusing to visit her parents more often, she had foolishly robbed herself of precious time she could have spent with them. And by not granting Wade her forgiveness, she'd thought she could punish him, and all but reveled in the guilt she knew he carried.

She didn't deserve his love, she told herself miserably. He'd tried so many times to tell her he was sorry, begged her repeatedly for her forgiveness. Yet in spite of her spitefulness, when he'd found her crying over her father's letters, he'd comforted her. Offered her his ear, as well as his shoulder to cry on, when he'd insisted upon being with her when she read the letters that remained.

And what had she given him in return? she asked herself. Had she given him her forgiveness when he'd admitted making a mistake? Offered him her understanding when he'd shared with her his past? Her acceptance when he'd asked her to share his life with him and his daughter?

No, she thought, shaking her head sadly. She'd used his mistake like a battering ram to beat him with. Remained silent, horrified even, as he'd confessed to a past that still shamed him. And she'd refused his proposal to share his life with him, insisting that she needed time to come to grips with her resentment toward his daughter.

She'd promised she'd be his friend, told him that she loved him. But how could a woman who professed those things turn her back on a man when he most needed her understanding and her love?

She rose, the letter she'd been reading falling to the floor, forgotten. She had to talk to him, she told herself and hurried for the door. See him. Tell him that his past didn't matter. Grant him the full forgiveness that she'd selfishly withheld. And she would deal with her conflicting feelings for his daughter, she told herself as she climbed into her car. Perhaps even help him see that Meghan needed his discipline as much as she needed his love.

It didn't occur to Stephanie that Wade's ex-wife might still be at his house until she pulled to a stop and saw the strange car parked on the drive. For a moment she was tempted to turn around and return home. She didn't want to meet his ex, doubted she could look the woman in the face without wanting to claw her eyes out.

But she couldn't let another moment pass without sharing her heart with Wade. Stiffening her resolve, she climbed out.

In spite of the lateness of the hour, a light burned in the kitchen window. Hoping not to disturb the entire household, she walked around back. At the door she hesitated a moment, then squared her shoulders and knocked.

She jumped, startled, when the door was immediately snatched open and a woman appeared in the space.

Backlit by the overhead light in the kitchen, the woman's face was shadowed, but Stephanie had a feeling she was confronting Wade's ex-wife for the first time.

Gulping, she asked uneasily, "Is Wade here?"

"Who wants to know?"

Stephanie set her jaw at the woman's hostile tone. "Stephanie Calloway. I'm a neighbor."

The woman gave her a slow look up and down, then stepped back and shouted, "Wade! That snotty little bitch from next door is here to see you."

Stephanie stared, while shock and anger fought for dominance of her emotions. Managing to push both back, she jutted her chin and strode inside.

Wade's ex had moved to the sink and was standing with her hips braced against its edge, her lips pursed in a smirk. Bone-thin, she wore a shockingly short denim skirt and a low-cut tank top. Her breasts—obviously silicone-enhanced—were as large as grapefruits and looked totally out of proportion to her emaciated frame.

"Didn't your mother teach you any manners?" the woman snapped, making Stephanie jump. "It's rude to stare."

Her cheeks flaming, Stephanie tore her gaze away. "I'm sorry. I didn't mean to—"

"Steph?"

She spun to find Wade standing in the doorway that opened from the kitchen to the den. She sagged her shoulders, almost weak with relief at seeing him. "I'm sorry to barge in like this. I had no idea you had—"

The woman quickly shifted in front of Stephanie, blocking her view of Wade.

"Well, well, well," she said as she folded her arms

across her chest and gave Stephanie another slow look up and down. "Looks like I've screwed up your plans." She lifted a brow plucked pencil-thin and added pointedly, *"Again."*

"That's enough, Angela," Wade warned.

She kept her gaze on Stephanie and smiled. "Oh, I don't think so. In fact, I haven't even gotten started good yet. I've wanted to give this lady a piece of mind for years."

"Angela," he warned again and took a step toward her.

"What's wrong, sugar?" Though her eyes were fixed on Stephanie, her question was directed at Wade. "Afraid I'll say something you don't want Miss Goody Two-shoes to hear?"

Wade lunged and caught Angela's elbow, whirled her around. "I said enough, Angela," he said, then released her and pointed a stiff finger at the hall and the stairs beyond. "Now go upstairs before you make me do something we'll both regret."

She shoved her face within inches of his. "You can't tell me what to do. Not anymore. I followed your orders for six long years, while you tried to shape me into what you considered the perfect wife. Well, guess what, Wade?" She opened her arms wide. "I'm not perfect and I never was. Not even while I was pretending to be the Stepford wife you wanted me to be. While you were off working, I'd drop Meghan off at day care and drive to Austin and have me a good ol' time. Those college boys really know how to party. All the booze and drugs I wanted, and all they expected from me in return was a piece of my ass."

He grabbed for her again, but she ducked to the side,

managing to dodge him. "I like drugs and the way they make me feel," she said, then smiled and dragged a fingernail down between her breasts. "And I like sleeping with a different man every night, especially one who isn't grieving over some old flame."

"I'm warning you, Angela," Wade said, his face red with rage, "either you shut up or I'll fix it so you'll never see our daughter again."

"*Our* daughter?" she repeated, then dropped her head back and laughed, the sound so evil it sent a shiver chasing down Stephanie's spine.

"Meghan isn't *your* daughter," she said. "I just told you that so you'd have to marry me. You thought you could just up and leave me in Houston, taking all your money with you." She snorted a laugh. "Well, I showed you, didn't I? You and Miss Goody Two-shoes here had your future all planned out, but I messed things up for you good, didn't I, when I showed up in town pregnant out to here."

Wade grabbed her again, and this time Angela was too slow to dodge him. He all but dragged her from the room and to the stairs, with her kicking and cursing him every step of the way.

Stephanie stood as if her feet had rooted to the floor, sickened by the ugly scene she'd just witnessed, the infidelities Angela had confessed to. She remained there, a hand pressed to her stomach, forcing herself to take slow, deep breaths until the nausea slowly faded and only one statement remained to circle in her mind.

Meghan isn't your daughter.

She closed her eyes, hearing again the vindictiveness in Angela's voice, envisioning the hate it had carved into her features as she'd hurled the confession like a knife to pierce Wade's heart.

Wade, she thought, and her gaze went instinctively to the stairs, wondering if it was true that he wasn't Meghan's father. Angela might only have said that to hurt him. To punish him for the injustices she felt she'd suffered at his hand.

As she continued to stare at the spot where she'd last seen him, Wade appeared on the stairway, his steps slow, his shoulders stooped as if he was burdened beneath the weight of the world. She started toward him, then stopped and wrung her hands at her waist, unsure what to say to him, what to do.

"Wade?" she said hesitantly.

He glanced her way, held her gaze a moment, then continued down the stairs.

She watched, her breath burning a hole in her chest as he reached the end and turned toward her.

"I'm sorry you had to listen to all that. You didn't deserve to hear any of what she said."

She shook her head, unable to push a word past the emotion that clotted her throat. Catching his hands, desperate for that contact, she gave them a reassuring squeeze. "It's not your fault. I should've called first. It never even occurred to me that she might still be here. I was so anxious to see you, talk to you, I didn't think about anything else. When you didn't come by at noon, I went outside and found the box of letters on the porch. When I saw it, I knew it meant you didn't want to see me, that you probably wouldn't be coming by anymore."

Tears filled her eyes, and she stubbornly blinked them back.

"But it wasn't until earlier this evening, after I'd read one of my dad's letters, that I realized it was all my fault. I let you leave last night without telling you how I feel. I should have told you then that your past doesn't matter to me, that I love you with all my heart and that I want to marry you."

Throughout her speech, he had listened quietly, his gaze steady on hers. And now that she was done, had said everything that was in her heart, and he still said nothing, she felt a moment's unease.

"Wade?" she asked hesitantly. "Is something wrong?"

"You didn't mention Meghan. When I asked you to marry me, you said you needed time, that you didn't think you could live in my house with her there as a constant reminder of the past."

"Yes, I did say that, but that's not a problem anymore."

"Why? Because Angela said that Meghan isn't mine?"

Numbed by the chill in his voice, the steely gleam in his eye, she shook her head. "Well, no. Of course not. I—"

Pulling his hands from hers, he took a step back. "What Angela said was true…to a point. Until the day Meghan was born, I did think she was mine. But when the nurse told me that Meghan weighed only four pounds and was considered a preemie, I knew that Angela had lied and was trying to stick me with another man's child.

"But here's a news flash for you, Steph," he continued. "It didn't matter. Not to me. Not then, and it sure as hell doesn't now. From the moment that doctor put Meghan in my arms she was mine. There was no way I was going to walk away from that baby and leave her with Angela to raise. I knew what kind of person Angela was, how she lived. And I knew that was the kind of life Meghan would have if I walked out on her. That's why when I divorced Angela I fought so hard for custody of Meghan."

Shaking his head, he took another step back, putting even more distance between him and Stephanie. "But it was more than Angela's lifestyle that made me want to keep Meghan with me. I love that girl as if she were my own. And because I love her, I would never marry a woman who didn't love her as much I do, who wasn't willing to put Meghan's happiness above her own. That's what parents do, Steph. They love their children unconditionally. Even when that child is not their own flesh and blood."

He turned and walked away.

Stephanie made the short drive home, her eyes fixed on the road ahead, her hands gripped tightly around the steering wheel. The tears were there in her throat, behind her eyes, yet she couldn't cry. She needed to. Oh, God, how she needed to.

She'd lost him. She'd allowed her resentment and bitterness to cost her a second chance to be with the one man she'd ever loved.

She didn't deserve to cry, she told herself. Didn't deserve the release it offered, the emptying of all emotion. She'd let him down. The man who had freely and generously offered to share everything he cherished most in the world—his heart, his daughter, his home— she'd let him down when he'd needed her most.

She understood now why he'd become so angry with

her for referring to Bud by his given name rather than her usual "Dad," and for what he considered her careless disregard of Bud's favorite possessions. He was bound to have seen himself in Bud, as they'd both raised daughters that weren't their own, and he'd probably feared that someday Meghan might find her real father and transfer her affection and allegiance to him, as Wade had thought Stephanie had transferred hers to her biological father.

Wade was wrong, though. Stephanie's determination to get to know her real father in no way changed how she felt about Bud. He was the only father she had ever known. He'd raised her, cared for her, loved her, and she would always love him. He was her father in every way but blood, and nothing would ever change that.

But she'd never have the chance to tell Wade that. She'd let him down, and now he was gone from her life forever.

For two days Stephanie packed like a wild woman, managing to accomplish more in that short space of time than she had in the entire previous week. Twice she saw Wade drive by the house on his way to check on the cattle, and though she watched from the window, praying with all her heart that he would stop, he passed by without so much as glancing toward the house. Each time, her heart would sink a little lower in her chest, and she would resume her packing, more determined than ever to finish the job and return to Dallas, putting as much distance as possible between her and the memories that haunted her.

On the third day, with most of the packing complete,

she placed a call to Bud's attorney and scheduled an appointment for that afternoon, then phoned a moving company and made arrangements to have the items she planned to save picked up on Friday and hauled to a storage facility in Dallas.

As she walked through the house on her way to her bedroom to shower and dress for her appointment with the attorney, an indescribable sadness slipped over her. The walls she passed were blank, save for the occasional rectangle of brighter paint where a picture had once hung. Boxes and furniture lined the walls and segmented the rooms, creating walkways that led from one room to the other. By Friday afternoon the house would be completely empty, listed for sale, and within a few short months, according to the Realtor she'd spoken to, a new owner would be moving in.

At the doorway to her bedroom she stopped and looked back down the hall, her heart breaking a little at the thought of another family living in the house she'd considered home for most of her life. Closing her eyes, she could almost hear the sounds that had once filled the house. The slam of the back door and Bud's voice as he called his standard greeting of, "When's dinner? I'm starving." The bark of the dog that always followed him in. Her mother fussing, "Wipe your feet, Bud Calloway! I just mopped that floor." The whir of the box fan that Bud kept aimed at his recliner in the summer months to keep him cool. The steady ticktock, ticktock of the clock that had sat on the fireplace mantel for more years than Stephanie could remember. Bud's soft call of, "'Night, Stephie," as he passed by her door on the way to his room.

Dragging an arm across the moisture that filled her eyes, she turned into her bedroom.

Stephanie settled in the chair opposite the lawyer's desk and offered Mr. Banks, Bud's attorney, a smile. "I appreciate you making time for me on such short notice."

He waved away her thanks. "No problem. I know you're anxious to get back to your own home and your work."

Stephanie released a long breath. "Yes, I am."

Getting down to business, Banks shuffled through the papers on his desk, then passed Stephanie a sheaf of papers he pulled from the stack. "A copy of Bud's will," he explained, then settled back in his chair, holding his own copy before him. "Most of this is standard language and the bequeaths what you'd expect, so I'll only bring to your attention the things I think might overly concern you or that you might question the validity of."

Stephanie looked at him curiously. "Why would I question anything? I'm familiar with Bud's wishes. He gave me a copy of his will shortly after Mom passed away."

Mr. Banks averted his gaze. "Well, uh—" He cleared his throat. "Well, you see, uh, Bud made a few changes."

A chill of premonition chased down Stephanie's spine. "What kind of changes?"

He flapped a hand, indicating the papers she held. "If you'll turn to page six, paragraph three." While she flipped pages, looking for the spot mentioned, he went on to explain, "As Bud's only child, you inherit everything. All stocks, bonds, insurance policies, the house and all its contents." He paused to clear his throat, then added, "But Bud left the land to Wade Parker."

Stunned, Stephanie could only stare. "He left the ranch to Wade?"

His expression grim, Banks nodded. "I know you must be shocked to learn this and I regret that it's my duty to deliver the news. I tried to get Bud to talk to you about it before he made the change, but he refused. Said he couldn't."

Stephanie choked out a laugh as the irony of the bequest set in. "No, Bud would never have mentioned Wade's name to me."

Banks leaned forward, his face creased with sympathy. "I'm sorry to be the one to tell you all this," he said with real regret. "I can only imagine how upsetting it must be for you. But I assure you, Bud was in sound mind when he made the change. I would never have done what he asked if I hadn't been absolutely sure he was sane."

Stephanie offered Banks a soft smile, hoping to ease his concern. "You needn't worry. I have no intention of contesting Bud's will. He knew that I wasn't interested in the land or in returning to Georgetown. Giving the land to Wade was his way of seeing that his ranch remained intact and wasn't cut up into a subdivision."

"He did mention that he feared that was what would happen to the place if it were ever put up for sale."

Rising, Stephanie extended her hand. "Thank you, Mr. Banks. I appreciate your concern for me. I truly do. But you can rest assured that I will honor Bud's wishes and will do nothing to stand in the way of Wade obtaining the deed to my father's ranch."

* * *

Late that night, unable to sleep, Stephanie sat on the front porch swing, slowly swaying back and forth, thinking over what Bud had done. Mr. Banks had been right when he'd assumed that Stephanie would be shocked by the discovery. She was more than shocked. She was stunned.

But that had lasted only a moment or two. She knew better than anyone how much Bud had loved his ranch, and it made perfect sense to her that he would want someone to have it who would love it as much as he had. Not that Stephanie didn't have strong feelings about the home where she was raised. She did. But she'd never made a secret of the fact that she had no desire to ever live there again. The truth was, she'd avoided coming home most of her adult life. Even though that must have hurt Bud, he had never held it against her. He'd loved her unconditionally throughout his life and, after his death, had generously left her with everything that was his, with the exception of his land.

Wade was the natural choice to receive the ranch. He would honor the gift and care for the land as much—if not more than—Bud had, and certainly more than Stephanie ever would. He'd already proved his dependability by taking care of things for Bud when Bud's health had declined, making it difficult, if not impossible, for him to do his chores himself. The gift to Wade was a large one, the value of the land alone worth probably close to a million dollars. But Wade would never sell the land to get the money it would bring. He had plenty of his own.

Closing her eyes, Stephanie examined her heart,

searching for any signs of resentment or bitterness toward Wade for receiving something that by all rights should have been hers. Oddly she felt nothing but a swell of pride that Bud had thought enough of Wade to give him something that had meant so much to him.

Sighing, she laid her head back and pushed a bare toe against the floor of the porch, setting the swing into motion again. Tomorrow the movers would come, she reminded herself, and she would be returning to Dallas and her own home.

She remembered when she'd first arrived to clean out her parents' house, she'd been anxious to close this chapter of her life once and for all and return to Dallas and her home there.

Now the mere thought of leaving made her want to cry.

Eight

Runt's sharp bark all but snatched Stephanie from a deep sleep and into a sitting position on the bed. Her heart thumping, she looked around.

"What is it, Runt?" she whispered.

He barked again, then trotted to the bedroom door.

Stephanie swung her legs over the side of the bed and grabbed her robe, pulling it on. Just as she reached the door, she heard a loud pounding.

"Steph? Open up! It's me. Wade."

Fully awake now, she flung open her bedroom door and ran down the hall, dodging boxes as she passed through the den. When she reached the front door, she fumbled the lock open, then flipped on the porch light as she swung the door wide, sure that he had come to reconcile with her.

Seeing the worry that etched his face, she wrapped

her robe more tightly around her and stepped outside. "What's wrong? Has something happened?"

"It's Meghan. She's gone. She was in bed asleep not more than four hours ago and now she's gone."

"Are you sure?"

"Of course I'm sure," he shouted impatiently. "I've searched the house, the barn, and there's no sign of her anywhere. I thought maybe she had come over here."

"Here?" she repeated, stunned that he would think Meghan would run away to her house.

Dragging a hand over his hair, he paced in front of her. "She likes you. Was mad when I wouldn't let her come back over and help you pack."

Stephanie gulped, unaware that Meghan had felt anything toward her, much less affection. Gathering the collar of her robe to her neck, she shook her head. "I haven't seen her. Have you called any of her friends."

"No. I hated to wake people up in the middle of the night until I was sure she was missing. I was so sure I'd find her here." He stopped and dropped his head back. "Oh, God," he moaned, his face contorted with what looked like pain. "She's gone to Angela's. I know she has."

Stephanie shuddered at the very suggestion, understanding Wade's concern, then set her jaw, knowing one of them had to remain calm. "You don't know that she has. Have you called Angela? Maybe she's talked to Meghan, knows where she is."

"I tried. She didn't answer, which doesn't surprise me." He scowled. "She was mad at me when she left the other day."

"How she feels about you isn't important right now,"

Stephanie reminded him firmly. "Meghan's safety is what you need to focus on. Now think. Where would she go? Who would she call?"

Wade tossed up his hands. "Hell, I don't know! When she's threatened to run away in the past, it's always been to her mother's. There isn't any other place I can think of where she'd go."

"Houston is almost three hours from here," Stephanie said, trying to think things out. "She couldn't very well walk there." Her eyes sharpened. "The bus station," she said and grabbed Wade's arm, shoving him toward his truck. "She'd probably catch a bus. Check there. Show her picture around. See if anyone remembers seeing her."

Wade dug in his heels. "But she'd have to get to town first."

Stephanie yanked open the door of his truck. "She could've walked. Hitchhiked. How she got there isn't important, and the more time you waste, the colder her trail is going to grow." She gave him a push. "Go! Find her and bring her home."

His expression grim, Wade started the ignition. "If she shows up here or contacts you—"

"I'll call you on your cell," she said, cutting him off. "And you call me if you find her."

Nodding, he slammed the door and gunned the engine and drove off with a squeal of tires.

Hugging her arms around her waist, Stephanie moved to stand in the middle of the drive and watched until his taillights disappeared from sight.

Drawing a deep breath, she turned for the house, knowing she wouldn't get a wink of sleep until she knew Meghan was safe and praying that Meghan was with one of her girlfriends and not on her way to Houston and Angela's house.

Her eyes burning from lack of sleep and her nerves tingling with worry, Stephanie walked through the house, directing the movers as they loaded the furniture and the boxes she'd marked as keepers.

Wade had called around four o'clock that morning to let her know that Meghan had bought a bus ticket for Houston and he was on his way there, hoping to intercept her before she reached Angela's. Since then, the phone had remained frustratingly silent.

She wanted desperately to call him, but each time she reached for the phone, she pulled her hand back, telling herself that he would contact her if there was any news.

Her nerves shot, she watched the movers load the last piece of furniture into the van. "I gave you the address of the storage facility, right?" she asked.

The driver patted his pocket. "Yes, ma'am. Got it right here."

She forced a smile. "Okay, then. I guess you're all set."

He lifted a hand in acknowledgment, then climbed behind the wheel while his partner hopped up onto the passenger seat on the opposite side.

With nothing left for her to do, Stephanie returned to the house and closed the front door behind her. The sound echoed hollowly in the empty house. She looked around, unsure what to do. One of the local charities had sent a truck by earlier in the day to pick up the items she had opted to donate. All that remained to signify the passing of her parents' lives was the huge pile of trash bags out back, and that, too, would be gone by morning, as she'd made arrangements with a garbage company to have it hauled off.

She'd originally planned to leave right after the moving van pulled out. Her bag was already packed and propped by the back door. But she couldn't leave now. Not with Meghan still missing. Worried that the phone company had misunderstood her instructions and shut off the phone today, rather than next week as she'd requested, she hurried to the kitchen and picked up the phone to make sure it was still working. Hearing the buzz of the dial tone, she replaced the receiver quickly, fearing she'd miss Wade's call.

"No news is good news," she reminded herself. Finding no consolation in the old adage, she began to pace—and nearly jumped out of her skin when the phone rang.

Leaping for it, she snatched the receiver to her ear. "Hello?"

"She's not at Angela's. Nobody is."

She pressed her fingers to her lips, her heart breaking at the defeat she heard in Wade's voice. "What are you going to do now?"

"I'm staying here. I know a couple of Angela's old hangouts, people she used to run around with. I'm going to make the rounds, find out if anybody has seen her."

"But what if Meghan comes back home? If you're gone, she might leave again."

"I was hoping you would go over there. Keep her there until I could get back."

"Of course I will."

"There's a key under the mat at the back door."

"I'll find it."

She started to hang up, but Wade's voice stopped her. "Steph?"

She pressed the phone back to her ear. "Yes?"

"Thanks."

Tears filled her eyes, but before she could respond, the dial tone buzzed in her ear, letting her know that he'd broken the connection.

Stephanie felt odd being in Wade's house. She was familiar with his home's layout, as she'd spent a lot of time there the summer they'd dated, but she chose to remain in the kitchen and near the phone hanging on the wall.

She made a pot of coffee to keep herself awake and drained cup after cup while sitting at the table. The clock on the oven recorded a digital time of 10:00 p.m., reminding Stephanie that she'd been at his house for over four hours.

The phone rang, startling her, and she lunged for it, catching it on the second ring.

"Hello?" she said breathlessly.

"Wade Parker, please."

Disappointed that it wasn't Wade calling, she brushed the hair back from her face. "I'm sorry, but he isn't in right now. Can I take a message?"

"No, I need to speak with him directly."

She frowned, wondering at the insistency in the man's voice. "I have his cell number. Would you like to try that?"

"I've already tried his cell. The call went straight to his voice mail. Hang on a second."

Her frown deepening, she listened, trying to make out what was being said, but whoever was on the other end of the line had covered the mouthpiece with his hand.

"Who am I talking to?"

Surprised by the question, she said, "Stephanie Calloway. I'm a neighbor."

"Just a sec."

Again the man covered the mouthpiece. Stephanie tightened her hand on the receiver, wondering if the call had something to do with Meghan.

"There's a young girl here who wants to speak to you," the man said.

The next voice Stephanie heard was Meghan's.

"Stephanie?" she said and sniffed. "Do you know where my daddy is?"

Fearing Meghan would hang up before Stephanie found out where she was, she said, "Where are you, Meghan? Your father is worried sick."

Meghan sniffed again, then said tearfully, "At the police station. In Austin."

Stephanie's eyes shot wide. A thousand questions crowded her tongue, but she couldn't ask them. Now was not the time. "Sweetheart, your daddy is in Houston looking for you."

Meghan burst into tears, and Stephanie had to swallow hard to keep from crying, too. "Meghan, listen to me," she said firmly. "Is the man with you a police officer?"

"Y-yes, ma'am."

"Let me speak to him."

"Okay. Stephanie?"

"Yes, sweetheart?"

"Will you come and get me?"

"Oh, honey," Stephanie moaned, her heart breaking at the pleading in the girl's voice. "I don't know if they'll release you to me. I'm not family."

"Please," Meghan begged and began to cry again. "I'm so scared."

"I'm on my way," Stephanie said quickly, having to raise her voice to be heard over Meghan's sobbing. "Give the phone back to the police officer so he can give me directions."

It was Stephanie's first visit to a police station…and she prayed it was her last. She supposed it could be the lateness of the hour that made the place appear so spooky, but she wouldn't bet on it. People—hoodlums, judging by their appearance—lounged outside the building and stood in loose groups in the hallway inside. Hugging her purse to her side for fear one of the thugs eyeing her would snatch it, she approached the desk.

"I'm here to see Meghan Parker," she told the officer on duty.

He looked at her, his expression bored. "You family?"

"No. A friend."

He shook his head. "We can only release her to a family member."

She bit down on her temper. "I'm aware of that, but she's just a child and she's frightened. I only want to stay with her until her father can get here."

He lifted a brow. "He's on his way? Last I heard, he couldn't be reached."

Anxious to see Meghan, she balled her hands to keep herself from throttling the man. "That's true, but I've left him a message on his cell phone and I'm sure as soon as he receives it he'll get here as quickly as he can. Now may I please see Meghan?"

With a shrug he stood and motioned her to follow him. He led her down a long hall and stopped before a door marked Interview and gave her a warning look. "Don't try sneaking her out. You'll only get yourself thrown in jail. She's a minor and can only be released to a family member."

She burned him with a look. "You needn't worry. I have an aversion to jails and have no intention of staying here a second longer than is necessary." Pushing past him, she opened the door.

Meghan was stretched out on a grouping of chairs, her face buried in the crook of her arm. She looked so small lying there. So incredibly young.

"Meghan?" Stephanie called softly.

Meghan sat up, blinked. Her eyes rounded when she saw Stephanie, then she shot off the chairs and into Stephanie's arms.

"Oh, Stephanie," she sobbed. "I was so scared you wouldn't come."

"Shh," Stephanie soothed. "There's no need to cry. I'm here and I'm going to stay with you until your dad arrives. Now why don't you tell me what happened? Why did you run away?"

Meghan's sobs grew louder. "Mom said Daddy didn't want me anymore. That I wasn't his. She told me to go to the bus station and buy a ticket to Houston. I did, but then she came to the station and got me. Said the ticket was just to fool dad. She took me to Austin and to a friend of her's house. It was awful," she cried and clung tighter to Stephanie. "People were snorting coke and doing all kinds of bad things.

"I begged her to leave. Take me somewhere else. But she wouldn't. She told me to shut up and have some fun for a change. I was so scared. These men kept looking at me all weirdlike. So I went into the bathroom and locked the door."

Stephanie stroked a hand down Meghan's hair, horrified to think of what might have happened to Meghan, the danger her mother had placed her in. "That was a very smart thing for you to do."

"I thought so, too. But then the police came and started beating on the door. Only I didn't know it was the police. I was crying and screaming for them to go away, and they beat the door down. I tried to tell the cop that I didn't want to be there, that my mother had brought me and made me stay. But he wouldn't listen. Said I had to go with him, that he couldn't leave me there alone. He made me get into the back of a police car with a couple of other people and brought me here."

Stephanie tried to block the awful images that rose in her mind. The kind of people that Meghan would've been sequestered with. The things she'd seen at that house. What might've happened to her if the police hadn't arrived when they had. Squeezing her eyes shut, she made herself focus on what Meghan was saying.

"When we got here, this woman cop brought me to this room. I gave them Daddy's name and number. She called him, but he wasn't home. So I gave them his cell number, but he didn't answer it either."

"I tried to call him, too, sweetheart," Stephanie told her. "His battery must be dead or he's out of range."

Gathering Meghan beneath her arm, she moved her toward the chairs. "But he'll come as soon as he gets the message."

Meghan sat, her eyes round with fear and fixed on Stephanie. "What if he doesn't?" Tears welled in her eyes. "Maybe he doesn't want me anymore. Mom said he didn't."

Stephanie pulled her into her arms. "That's not true. Your father loves you very much."

"But that's just it," Meghan sobbed. "He's not my father. Mom lied to him. She said she told him she was pregnant and the baby was his so he'd have to marry her."

Stephanie set her jaw hard enough to crack a tooth and hugged Meghan tighter against her chest. "I don't care what your mother told you. Wade loves you. Don't you ever doubt that for a minute."

Swearing, Wade yanked his battery charger from the adapter on his dash and hurled it out the window. Of all times for the stupid thing to break, this had to be the worst. He dragged a hand down his face and focused on the road, trying to think what to do. Seeing a gas station up ahead, he wheeled his truck into the parking lot and braked to a stop in front of a pay phone hanging on the side of the building.

Jumping out, he fished a quarter from his pocket, fed it into the slot, then punched in his cell phone number, silently praying Stephanie had called and left him a message telling him Meghan was home. When the recorded message started, asking him to leave a message, he quickly punched in the numerical code to take him directly to his voice mail. Pressing the phone to his ear, he listened. "Oh, no," he moaned and braced a hand against the wall to hold himself upright while he listened to a man, who identified himself as an Austin police officer, inform him that his daughter, Meghan Parker, was currently being held at the Austin Police Department on Seventh Street.

Wiping a shaky hand over his brow, he waited for the next message to begin.

"Wade, it's Stephanie. I talked to Meghan and she's at the Austin Police Department on Seventh Street, right off I-35. She's fine," she added quickly, "though understandably scared. I'm leaving now to go and stay with her. They won't release her to me, so you need to get to Austin as soon as possible."

Swearing, he dropped the receiver and jumped back into his truck. He was going to kill Angela, he told himself. If he ever got his hands on her, he was going to wring her lying neck. He knew she was behind this. How she'd pulled it off, he didn't know. But if Meghan was at a police station, Angela was the one responsible for her being there.

The door of the interview room flew open and Wade rushed in. He took one look at Meghan curled against Stephanie's side, then whipped his gaze to Stephanie's, the blood draining from his face.

Realizing that he thought Meghan was hurt, she shook her head. "She's fine," she whispered. "Just exhausted."

Meghan lifted her head and blinked. "Daddy?" she murmured sleepily. Tears filled her eyes when she saw Wade, and her face crumpled. "Oh, Daddy. I'm so sorry."

Wade crossed the room in two strides and gathered

her up in his arms, fitting her legs around his waist. "It's okay, baby," he soothed, then had to bury his face in her hair and gulp back his own tears. "Thank God you're all right. That's all that matters. You're safe."

Meghan clung tighter to him. "I just want to go home, Daddy. Please take me home."

"Don't worry, sweet cheeks," he assured her and headed for the door. "I've already cleared things with the police. We're good to go." He stopped at the doorway, as if only then remembering Stephanie was there, and glanced back, a brow lifted in question. "Do you need a ride?"

Stephanie rose, realizing that now that Wade and his daughter were reunited, her services were no longer needed. Though she should have been relieved that all had seemingly turned out well, she felt an inexplicable sadness.

She forced a smile. "No, I have my car."

Stephanie debated her options as she drove north on I-35 toward Georgetown, relieved to be leaving Austin behind. She was too tired to drive all the way to her home in Dallas, yet there was no place for her to sleep at her parents' house. All of the furniture had either been hauled away by the charitable group she'd donated it to or was currently sitting in a storage facility in Dallas.

Seeing a sign for a motel at the next exit, she slowed, considering stopping and getting a room. She sped up and passed the exit by, deciding that after the night she'd just spent, she needed the comfort and familiarity of her parents' home, even if it did mean she'd have to sleep on the floor.

Upon arriving, she parked beneath the shade of a tree near the back door rather than hassle with raising the garage door, Climbing out, she moaned softly as she stretched out the kinks sitting so long had left in her body. Hoping to find something she could use as bedding, she opened the rear doors of her SUV and dug through the items she kept stored there. She found a paper-thin blanket in the bag of emergency gear, tucked it under her arm, then dug around some more until she unearthed the inflatable neck pillow she used when traveling on airplanes. As an afterthought, she picked up the box containing her father's letters and headed for the house.

Once inside, she walked from room to room, feeling like Goldilocks as she searched for the most comfortable place to sleep. Deciding that the carpet in her bedroom was the cushiest, she set the box on the floor, then sank down beside it and blew up the neck pillow. Satisfied that she'd done all she could to make herself comfortable, she stretched out on her side, tucked the neck pillow beneath her cheek and drew the thin blanket up over her shoulder.

She released a long, exhausted breath, drew in another…and slept.

"Daddy?"

"Yeah?"

"Mom said that you and Stephanie used to be engaged."

Wade tensed, then forced his fingers to relax on the wand he held and twisted, closing the blinds and blocking out as much sunlight as possible from Meghan's room so that she could get some rest. "Yeah, we were."

"Mom said she broke y'all up so that you'd have to marry her."

Adding yet another item to the long list of reasons Meghan had already given him during the drive home to despise his ex, Wade crossed to sit down on the side of his daughter's bed. "In a way, I guess she did," he replied, not wanting to burden her with the details.

Tears welled in her eyes. "It was my fault, wasn't it? Because Mom was pregnant with me, you had to break your engagement to Stephanie."

He leaned to brush her hair back from her face. "No, sweet cheeks," he assured her. "The fault was mine. You had no part in it."

"You still like her, don't you? Stephanie, I mean."

He smiled sadly and drew his hand to cup her cheek. "Yeah. I guess I always will."

"You could still get married, couldn't you? I mean, it's not like you're married to Mom anymore."

He dropped his gaze, not sure how to answer. "It's more complicated than that."

She pulled herself up to sit, dropping her arms between her spread knees. "How?"

He hesitated, searching for a way to explain why he couldn't marry Stephanie that wouldn't make his daughter feel as if she were to blame. "Marriage is a big commitment," he began.

She rolled her eyes. "Duh. Like I don't already know that."

Chuckling, he scrubbed a hand over her hair. "If you're so smart, then you tell me why I *should* marry her."

"Because she's a hottie."

He choked out a laugh. "Hottie?" He shook his head. "Only a shallow man marries a woman for her looks."

"That's not the only reason," she said drily, then lifted a hand and began to tick off items. "She's smart, hip and really, really nice." She dropped her hands, her eyes filling with tears. "She came all the way to Austin to stay with me because I was scared. And she held me real tight when I cried, just like a real mom would. She made me feel safe, loved. Even knowing how bad I'd been, she didn't yell at me or anything. She was just...nice."

Wade stared, wondering if Stephanie's kindness to Meghan was a sign that she no longer resented his daughter. "Meghan?" he said hesitantly. "If Stephanie and I were to get married, she would become your step-mother. How would you feel about that?"

Meghan frowned, as if she hadn't considered that aspect, then smiled. "I think that would be really cool."

"Are you sure? Now think about this before you answer," he warned. "She'd be living in our house with us, and I'm sure she'd have her own set of rules she'd expect us to follow. Consequences, too," he added, re-membering his conversation with Stephanie about cursing.

She drew back, eyeing him warily. "Gosh, Dad. You make her sound like some kind of witch."

He shrugged. "I just want to make sure that you un-derstand that if Stephanie and I were to marry, I would expect you to give her the respect any mother deserves."

She lifted a brow and looked down her nose at him. "*Any* mother?"

He rolled his eyes, knowing she was referring to Angela. "You know what I mean."

"I will. I promise." She gave him a push. "Go and ask her. I'll bet she says yes."

He gaped. "Now?"

She flopped to her back and pulled the covers to her chin. "Why not? It's not like you have anything better to do."

He rose slowly, fighting a sudden attack of nerves. "No, I guess I don't."

Wade wasn't sure if he'd find Stephanie at her parents' house, but he figured that was as good a place as any to start his search.

He prayed it was a good sign when he found her SUV parked beneath the shade tree near the back. Unsure how she'd respond to another proposal, he crossed to the front door and knocked. He waited, shifting nervously from foot to foot. When he didn't receive a response, he lifted a hand above the door and felt along the edge for the key. Finding it, he unlocked the door and let himself in.

He glanced around and was shocked to see that the house was empty, not a stick of furniture or a box in sight. Realizing that Steph had completed the job she'd come to do and would be leaving soon made his stomach twist with dread.

Runt trotted out from the kitchen and bumped his nose against Wade's hand.

"Hey, Runt," he said and gave the dog a distracted pat as he looked around. "Where's Steph?"

In answer, the dog started down the hall. Wade followed, his hands slick with sweat, his throat dry as a bone.

At the door of her bedroom Runt dropped down on his haunches and looked up expectantly at Wade.

"Good boy," Wade murmured and gave the dog a pat as he leaned to peek inside.

Guilt stabbed at him when he saw Steph asleep on the floor with only a blanket for cover. Silently kicking himself for not thinking to ask her to come to his house when they'd left the police station, he tiptoed into the room and sank down to his knees at her side.

"Steph?" he whispered and gave her arm a nudge.

She moaned softly and pulled the blanket over her head. "Not now, Runt," she complained. "I'm sleeping."

Biting back a smile, Wade stretched out on his side to face her. Careful not to startle her, he lifted the edge of the blanket. "It's not Runt, Steph," he whispered. "It's me. Wade."

She blinked open her eyes. Blinked again, then tensed. "Is Meghan okay? Has something happened to her?"

He laid a hand against her cheek, touched by the alarm and concern in her voice. "She's fine. When I left, she was sleeping."

Obviously relieved, she closed her hand over his and let her lids drift down. "Good. Poor baby was tired."

Poor baby. Hearing her use that one endearment told Wade all he needed to know. He eased his body closer to hers. "Steph? I need for you to wake up."

"Tired," she moaned. "So tired."

"I know you are, sunshine, but there's something I need to ask you."

"Can't it wait?" she complained.

Chuckling, he placed a finger on her eyelid and forced it up. "No, it can't," he told her firmly.

Heaving a sigh, she rolled to her back and scrubbed her hands over her face. "What?" she asked wearily.

He sat up in order to better see her. "I wanted to thank you for going to Austin and staying with Meghan until I could get there. That meant a lot to me."

Yawning, she rolled back to her side and pulled the blanket over her shoulder. "You're welcome."

"Meghan sends her thanks, too."

"Poor baby," she murmured sympathetically. "I can't imagine how frightened she must have been."

Because he knew only too well the kind of horrors his ex had subjected his daughter to, Wade scowled. "Yeah, she was scared all right." Heaving a sigh, he focused on Steph's face again. "Meghan said that you were really nice to her. Held her tight, like a real mom would."

Though her eyes remained closed, a tender smile curved Steph's lips. "That's really sweet. She's a good kid."

"You think so?"

Something in his voice must have caught her attention, because Steph opened her eyes and looked up at him. "Yes, I do."

"You said before that you didn't think you could live in the same house with her. Do you still feel that way?"

Her gaze on his, she slowly pushed herself up to an elbow. "Wade, what are you saying?"

He dipped his chin, shrugged. "Meghan and I had a little talk before I came here. She seems to think we should get married."

Her eyes shot wide. "Meghan said that?"

"Yeah. Angela told her that we were engaged before,

and Meghan was worried that it was her fault that our engagement was broken."

She shifted to sit and dropped her face onto her hands. "Oh, no," she moaned. "That is so unfair, so wrong. Angela should never have said that to her. Meghan wasn't to blame."

"Don't worry. I straightened Meghan out. I told her it was my fault, that she had nothing to do with it."

She opened her hands enough to peek at him. "And she believed you?"

He lifted a brow. "What choice did she have? It's kind of hard to argue with the truth. It *was* my fault."

She dropped her hands to frown. "No, it wasn't. It was Angela's."

He lifted a shoulder. "No matter who was to blame, I don't regret the decision I made. I only have to look at Meghan and know I did the right thing."

"Oh, Wade," she said, her face crumpling. "After all that woman put you through, you never once turned your back on Meghan."

"And I never will," he said firmly. He caught her hand and squeezed. "And I hope you won't either."

Her tears welled higher. "I won't. I couldn't."

He gulped and gripped her hands more tightly. "There's something you need to know. Something that might make you angry. I probably should've mentioned it before, but I didn't think it was my place."

A soft smile curved her lips. "If it's about Bud leaving you his land, you needn't worry. I already know."

His eyes widened in surprise. "You knew?"

"I met with Bud's lawyer. He told me."

"And you're not mad?"

She shook her head. "No. Surprised, yes, but not mad. Bud willed you his land because he knew you would love it as much as he did." She sputtered a laugh. "And I wouldn't be surprised if he didn't do it in hopes it would bring us together."

Smiling, he nodded. "That sounds like something Bud would do." Growing solemn, he shifted to kneel before her and brought her hands to his lips. "Stephanie Calloway, would you do me the honor of marrying me and becoming my wife?"

She stared at him as if afraid this was a dream she would wake from.

"Will you?" he prodded.

Laughing, she flung her arms around his neck. "Yes, yes, a thousand times yes!"

He squeezed his arms tightly around her and buried his face in her hair. "I've waited so long to hear you say that," he murmured, then drew back to look deeply into her eyes. "We're going to be a family. You, me and Meghan."

A sharp bark had him glancing toward the doorway, where Runt sat, looking at him expectantly.

Smiling, he added, "And Runt." He turned to look at Steph again and the smile melted from his face. "I love you, Stephanie Calloway."

"No more than I love you, Wade Parker."

He framed her face between his hands. "We're going to make it this time. Nothing is ever going to separate us again."

"Nothing," she promised and lifted her face to his.

Epilogue

Stephanie turned her hand slowly, watching as light from the bedside lamp caught the emerald-cut diamond of her ring and made it shimmer. It was the same ring Wade had slipped on her finger almost thirteen years ago. His mother's ring. Two weeks after he'd placed it on her finger, she'd ripped the ring off and thrown it at him. Closing her eyes against the unwanted memory, she curled her fingers to her palm as if to protect the ring and silently vowed never to take it off again. Ever.

Sighing, she opened her eyes to look at the ring again, then dropped her hand and reached for the last stack of letters sitting on the bedside table. She'd read them, just as she'd promised herself she would, and only one remained before she could say she'd read them all. Slipping the last envelope from the stack, she pushed back the flap and pulled out the folded pages.

As she opened them, a torn piece of paper fell to her lap.

"What's this?" she murmured and picked it up to examine it. Finding a jumble of handwritten words on one side, she turned it over to look at the back. Impressed into the paper was a notary's seal and a woman's signature. *Helen Thompson.* Frowning at the unfamiliar name, she flipped the paper back over and tried again to make sense of the words. She quickly gave up. Whatever message was originally written on the piece had lost its meaning when the document was torn.

Hoping to find an explanation in her father's letter, she set the piece of paper aside and smoothed open the pages of the letter over her propped up knees.

Dearest Janine,

I'm enclosing part of a document that I want you to have. I have no idea if it'll ever be worth anything, but keep it somewhere safe, just in case. I never mentioned it to you before, but I honestly thought the guy who gave this to me was either crazy or drunk. Maybe I'd better explain.

The night before I left for 'Nam I was in a bar in Austin with the guys I was traveling with and this man came up to our table and offered to buy us all a drink. We invited him to join us and he told us that he'd had a son who was killed in Vietnam. It happened several years before, but I could tell the man was still grieving. Anyway, he said, now that his son was dead, he didn't have anybody to leave his ranch to and said he wanted to leave it to us. He wrote out this bill of sale, had each one of us sign it, then tore it into six pieces and gave each one of us a piece. He told us, when we got back from Vietnam, we were to put the pieces together and come claim our ranch.

Like I said, I don't know if anything will ever come of this, but I want you to have it, just in case I don't make it home. Kind of like insurance, I guess.

I've never really thought about dying, but lately it's been on my mind a lot. Maybe it's because I'm going to be a daddy. I don't know. I've been worrying how you and the baby would make it if something were to happen to me. You'd get money from the Army. I know that for sure. But what I don't know is if it would be enough to support you and the baby without you having to work. And I don't want you to have to worry about working or money or anything like that.

I want you to be able to devote yourself to being a mommy.

I hope I haven't depressed you by telling you all this. My only purpose in writing it all down is so that you can take advantage of this opportunity, if it should ever present itself. If something should happen to me, the other guys will know what to do and they'll contact you. You can trust them. They'll see that you get your fair share.

I'd better go. We're heading out early in the morning and moving to an area where there's been some trouble. The guys and I have already decided that we're going to kick butt and get this war over with so we can come home.

Love forever and ever,
Larry

Blinking back tears, Stephanie carefully refolded the letter, then picked up the torn piece of paper. Insurance, she thought sadly, turning the yellowed and ragged piece of paper between her fingers. Since Stephanie was unaware of her mother ever having received a windfall, she had to believe that her father's assumption was right. The man who had given him the piece of paper had either been drunk or crazy.

"You still awake?"

Stephanie glanced up to find Wade in the doorway. Though she'd agreed to stay in his house, she had refused to sleep in his bedroom with him until they were properly married. With his daughter in the house, she'd thought it only proper.

Smiling, she patted the spot on the bed beside her. "I was just reading the last of my father's letters."

He hopped up onto the bed and settled beside her, stretching his legs out next to hers. "So? How was it? Any new revelations?"

She frowned thoughtfully. "I don't know." She passed the torn piece of paper to him. "Take a look at this. It was inside the letter."

He studied first one side, then the other, then shrugged and passed it back. "What is it? Some kind of secret code?"

She laughed softly. "It looks like it, doesn't it?" Her smile faded and she shook her head. "He sent it to Mom and told her to keep it someplace safe. Said it was insurance, in case he didn't make it home."

He took the piece of paper back from her to look at it again, then snorted. "Sure doesn't look like an insurance policy to me."

"It's not. A man gave it to him the night before he left for Vietnam. Him and five other soldiers. It's like a deed, I guess. Supposedly his son died in Vietnam, and since he didn't have anyone to leave his ranch to, he wanted my father and his friends to have it."

He snorted a laugh. "What man in his right mad would give his ranch to six complete strangers?"

"My father thought the same thing. He said in the letter that he thought the guy had to be drunk or crazy to do something like that." Growing thoughtful, she rubbed the torn edge of the paper across her lips. "I wonder what happened to the other five men?" She glanced at Wade. "There's a chance that some of them, if not all, made it back home."

He lifted a shoulder. "You'd think so."

"Wade," she said as an idea begin to form in her mind. "Do you think it would be possible to locate those soldiers? Find out what happened to them? Maybe where they live?"

"I don't know," he said doubtfully. "That was— what?—thirty-five years ago?"

"Give or take a few months." Catching her lower lip between her teeth, she tried to think how to go about locating the men. "I could write a letter to the Army," she said, thinking aloud. "Find out the names of the men that were in Dad's unit at the time he was killed."

"Yeah," he agreed. "That would be a start."

"Wonder how many men there were?"

"In his unit, you mean?" At her nod, he shrugged. "I have no idea. A lot, I'd imagine."

She firmed her mouth in determination. "It doesn't matter. I don't care if I have to write a thousand letters, I'm going to track down the five men who have the other pieces of paper."

"You don't really think it has any value, do you? Even if the guy who gave it to them was serious, that was thirty-five years ago. A lot could have happened in that amount of time."

Smiling, she dropped a kiss on his cheek. "Doesn't matter. Not to me. The only thing I'm interested in is finding my father's friends."

"Would you mind waiting until after we're married to start your search?"

She looked at him curiously. "Why?"

He curled up close to her and nuzzled her neck. "Because I don't want anything distracting you from planning this wedding and causing a delay. Having you in my house and not in my bed is driving me crazy."

She slid down until her face was even with his. "Doesn't Meghan ever have sleepovers with her friends?"

A slow smile spread across his face as he realized what she was suggesting. "Yeah, she does. Remind me to call Jan tomorrow and set one up."

She drew back to peer at him in surprise. "Isn't that rather bold to ask if your daughter can spend the night at someone's house? Shouldn't the invitation come from Jan?"

He looped an arm around her waist and drew her to him. "Jan'll understand." His lips spread across hers in a smile. "She's a single parent, too."

* * * * *

Don't miss the next book in Peggy Moreland's
A PIECE OF TEXAS *series.*
Watch for
THE TEXAN'S CONVENIENT MARRIAGE,
available in July from Silhouette Desire.

SUMMER OF SECRETS

**This exciting trilogy
continues in May with**

STRICTLY LONERGAN'S BUSINESS

(SD #1724)

by *USA TODAY* bestselling author

MAUREEN CHILD

He'd never thought of his ever-efficient
assistant as a flesh-and-blood—desirable—
woman. Then the lights went out!

On Sale May 2006

And don't miss
SATISFYING LONERGAN'S HONOR,
available in June from Silhouette Desire.

Available at your favorite retail outlet!

Visit Silhouette Books at www.eHarlequin.com   SDSLB0506

Silhouette Desire
presents the latest
Westmoreland title from

BRENDA JACKSON

THE DURANGO AFFAIR

(SD #1727)

Durango Westmoreland's bachelor
days are numbered when an
unforgettable night of passion with
hazel-eyed Savannah Claiborne
results in a big surprise...and
a hasty trip to the altar.

On Sale May 2006

Available at your favorite retail outlet!

Visit Silhouette Books at www.eHarlequin.com SDTDA0506

If you enjoyed what you just read,
then we've got an offer you can't resist!

Take 2 bestselling love stories FREE!

Plus get a FREE surprise gift!

Clip this page and mail it to Silhouette Reader Service™

IN U.S.A.	**IN CANADA**
3010 Walden Ave.	P.O. Box 609
P.O. Box 1867	Fort Erie, Ontario
Buffalo, N.Y. 14240-1867	L2A 5X3

YES! Please send me 2 free Silhouette Desire® novels and my free surprise gift. After receiving them, if I don't wish to receive anymore, I can return the shipping statement marked cancel. If I don't cancel, I will receive 6 brand-new novels every month, before they're available in stores! In the U.S.A., bill me at the bargain price of $3.80 plus 25¢ shipping and handling per book and applicable sales tax, if any*. In Canada, bill me at the bargain price of $4.47 plus 25¢ shipping and handling per book and applicable taxes**. That's the complete price and a savings of at least 10% off the cover prices—what a great deal!! I understand that accepting the 2 free books and gift places me under no obligation ever to buy any books. I can always return a shipment and cancel at any time. Even if I never buy another book from Silhouette, the 2 free books and gift are mine to keep forever.

225 SDN DZ9F
326 SDN DZ9G

Name	(PLEASE PRINT)	
Address	Apt.#	
City	State/Prov.	Zip/Postal Code

Not valid to current Silhouette Desire® subscribers.

Want to try two free books from another series?
Call 1-800-873-8635 or visit www.morefreebooks.com.

* Terms and prices subject to change without notice. Sales tax applicable in N.Y.
** Canadian residents will be charged applicable provincial taxes and GST.
 All orders subject to approval. Offer limited to one per household.
 ® are registered trademarks owned and used by the trademark owner and or its licensee.

DES04R   ©2004 Harlequin Enterprises Limited

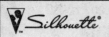

INTIMATE MOMENTS™

With the monarchy in upheaval,
who will capture Silvershire's crown?

FIND OUT IN INTIMATE MOMENTS'
NEW 6-BOOK *ROYALTY* SAGA FILLED WITH
GLAMOUR, PASSION AND BETRAYAL!

CAPTURING THE CROWN

THE HEART OF A RULER BY **MARIE FERRARELLA**
April 2006, #1412

THE PRINCESS'S SECRET SCANDAL
BY **KAREN WHIDDON**
May 2006, #1416

THE SHEIK AND I BY **LINDA WINSTEAD JONES**
June 2006, #1420

ROYAL BETRAYAL BY **NINA BRUHNS**
July 2006, #1424

MORE THAN A MISSION BY **CARIDAD PINEIRO**
August 2006, #1428

THE REBEL KING BY **KATHLEEN CREIGHTON**
September 2006, #1432

AVAILABLE WHEREVER YOU BUY BOOKS.

Visit Silhouette Books at www.eHarlequin.com SIMCTCLIST

ATHENA FORCE

**CHOSEN FOR THEIR TALENTS.
TRAINED TO BE THE BEST.
EXPECTED TO CHANGE THE WORLD.**

The women of Athena Academy are back.
Don't miss their compelling new adventures
as they reveal the truth about their founder's
unsolved murder—and provoke the wrath of a
cunning new enemy....

FLASHBACK
by Justine DAVIS

Available April 2006 at your favorite retail outlet.

MORE ATHENA ADVENTURES
COMING SOON:

Look-Alike by Meredith Fletcher, May 2006
Exclusive by Katherine Garbera, June 2006
Pawn by Carla Cassidy, July 2006
Comeback by Doranna Durgin, August 2006

www.SilhouetteBombshell.com   SBAF2006

THE OTHER WOMAN

by *Brenda Novak*

A Dundee, Idaho Book

Elizabeth O'Conner has finally put her
ex-husband's betrayal behind her. She's
concentrating on her two kids and on opening
her own business. One thing she's learned
is that she doesn't want to depend on any
man ever again—which definitely includes the
enigmatic Carter Hudson. It's just as well that
he's as reluctant to get involved as she is....

By the award-winning author of
Stranger in Town and *Big Girls Don't Cry.*

On sale May 2006
Available at your favorite retailer!

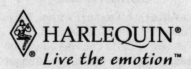

HARLEQUIN®
Live the emotion™

www.eHarlequin.com   HSRTOW0506

THE
ELLIOTTS

Mixing business with pleasure

continues with

MR. AND MISTRESS

(SD #1723)

HEIDI BETTS

She had been his kept woman...
until she discovered she was
pregnant with his child.
Did she dare reveal her
secret pregnancy?

On Sale May 2006

Available at your favorite retail outlet!

Visit Silhouette Books at www.eHarlequin.com SDMAM0506

COMING NEXT MONTH

#1723 MR. AND MISTRESS—Heidi Betts
The Elliotts
Scandal threatens to rock the Elliott family when a business mogul wants to make his pregnant mistress his wife!

#1724 STRICTLY LONERGAN'S BUSINESS—
Maureen Child
Summer of Secrets
She was his ever-dependent, quiet assistant…until a month of sharing close quarters finally allowed her to catch her boss's eye.

#1725 THE RAGS-TO-RICHES-WIFE—Metsy Hingle
Secrets Lives of Society Wives
After a secret rendezvous leads to an unplanned pregnancy, this Cinderella finds herself a high-society wife of convenience.

#1726 DEVLIN AND THE DEEP BLUE SEA—
Merline Lovelace
Code Name: Danger
He was a mystery to solve and she was just the woman to uncover *all* of his secrets!

#1727 THE DURANGO AFFAIR—Brenda Jackson
Having an affair with a man like Durango was like lighting a match during a drought—fast to ignite, hot to burn, impossible to quench.

#1728 HOUSE OF MIDNIGHT FANTASIES—Kristi Gold
Rich and Reclusive
Reading your boss's mind can lead to trouble…*especially* when you're the one he's fantasizing about.

SDCNM0406